A
Harlequin
Romance

OTHER

Harlequin Romances

by AMANDA DOYLE

Many of these titles are available at your local bookseller,
or through the Harlequin Reader Service.

For a free catalogue listing all available Harlequin Romances,
send your name and address to:

HARLEQUIN READER SERVICE,
M.P.O. Box 707, Niagara Falls, N.Y. 14302
Canadian address: Stratford, Ontario, Canada.

or use order coupon at back of book.

KOOKABURRA DAWN

by

AMANDA DOYLE

HARLEQUIN BOOKS   TORONTO
WINNIPEG

Original hard cover edition published in 1971
by Mills & Boon Limited, 17-19 Foley Street,
London W1A 1DR, England

© Amanda Doyle 1971

Harlequin edition published February, 1972

SBN 373-01562-3

Reprinted May, 1972

Printed in Canada

1562

As Renata Bentmore came down the hospital steps and made her way hurriedly towards the bus stop, she instinctively pulled the collar of her military-style raincoat closer about her neck with fingers which were chilled in spite of the black gloves that fitted like a second skin.

That was the way in which most of Rennie's apparel fitted.

She had the sort of slender, sinuous grace that could show figure-hugging fashions to their best advantage, which, coupled with her high cheekbones, smooth olive skin, and remarkably fine sherry brown eyes, probably accounted for her unmitigated success as one of London's most sought-after models.

Possibly her long blonde hair had something to do with her popularity, too. One glance at it had been enough for the photographers to label her as a 'natural' for the beachwear advertisements which she was already commissioned to do, shortly, for the third year in succession. As her slimly proportioned body became progressively browner in the sun, her abundant, straight fair tresses got fairer also, bleached to pale silken splendour without the slightest aid from bottle or hairdresser. When that happened, Rennie's sherry-coloured eyes seemed lighter, too. The gold of her skin was reflected in their dancing depths, capturing splinters of sunlight and mischief that could intrigue and entice without her even being aware of the fact.

Just now there was no sunlight – only a steady drizzle, sometimes whipped into stinging activity by the occasional gust of wind that swept along the street. When Rennie left the shelter of the houses to cross to the bus stop, that late summer wind slapped the thin rain against her cheeks and soaked the sheer nylons which she had thus far succeeded in keeping dry.

Damp and depressed as the weather itself, she stood in

the queue and reflected that a day such as this, in August, could be colder and drearier than winter itself. In December, there were at least warm street lamps, winking neon signs, bustling crowds of Christmas shoppers, floodlit shop windows to cheer one, and, appropriately booted, cosily muffled, one could even enjoy it.

Tonight, the light had faded to a misty pall that shrouded the spires of the city and wreathed the topmost branches of the black-trunked trees in the parks. Slated roofs were wet and dark, gutters dripped, drains gurgled, and tyres swished along the streets, throwing up a fine, dirty spray as the cars sped by.

Oh, no! It only needed that!

Rennie cursed softly beneath her breath, eyed her mud-spattered legs with a misgiving that was half tinged with amusement. In her bedraggled state, no one would ever suspect her professional status – not this evening.

She had received a number of curious glances since joining the queue. Rennie was accustomed to them by now, because her strongly boned features and faintly aquiline profile were bound to attract interest. Her face, she often thought half-regretfully, was almost too defined to be merely girlish. It matched her inclination to impulsive actions and snap decisions, her headstrong will, her love of open-air sports, her tendency to lead her fellows into well-intentioned causes that sometimes ended quite disastrously. She was a positive personality, that was the trouble. *Very* positive. Whatever Rennie chose to do, she did it with her entire heart and soul and mind and body, once the decision had been taken. Her sympathy for the underdog, the eagerness with which she supported lost causes, fought over principles, and fanned the dying sparks of fast-disappearing moral traditions against the current of modern opinion, had been something of a joke between herself and her father. Perhaps some of Professor Bentmore's idealism and unworldliness had, after all, rubbed off upon his high-spirited daughter, but whereas he had been able to sit apart and view the world from the remoteness of his tower of learning, to judge his fellow mortals with a sagacious impartiality and tolerance that

6

were at times almost tender, Rennie preferred to involve herself actively in impassioned outbursts and sometimes physical rebellion.

Her mouth curved tenderly now as she recalled her gentle, scholarly parent.

There had been a bond of closeness and understanding between them that even his unsuccessful second marriage had failed to destroy. Right up to the end, he had remained a devoted and affectionate father, fond even in those moments when he criticized her, an anchor of stability in Rennie's young, sometimes tempestuous world. He had been her confidante, her friend, until the final brief illness which had taken him from her. He had had a capacity for loving and giving which Rennie sometimes almost envied, until she saw that it could be a drawback as well as a benefit. For it was that same capacity which had involved him with Enid, which had blinded him to the woman's selfishness and blatantly mercenary designs, and which had made his last years such miserable ones, although he had been too loyal ever to admit the fact.

The loving-and-giving bit of her father's nature had been responsible for Rennie's present preoccupation with little Magda, too, she thought gloomily, as she was borne along on the small, jostling knot of people that surged towards the platform of the bus which had just arrived.

'Upstairs only. All upstairs now, please.'

Rennie gripped the rail as the vehicle lurched forward once more, and sank thankfully into the nearest vacant seat. From there she stared out on to the shiny wet tops of the cars which crawled along in the traffic beneath like so many coloured beetles, but she wasn't really seeing those cars at all just then – only Magda's small face, pale in the exposed places between the bandages.

Rennie turned away from the window.

It hurt her to think of Magda, sitting up in the children's ward, fondling the panda with its mended arm and single eye. It was one which Rennie herself had given her at the time of her first operation, and after all this time Magda still kept it by her side, caressing it with fingers that were still patient, and by now heartrendingly re-signed.

Three years had passed since the beginning of Magda's skin-grafting treatment, and this was her fifth spell in hospital – her fifth and *final* spell, Rennie had been assured by the plastic surgeon who had undertaken Magda's case – and she could only pray that it would be so, because each time that her little orphaned relative entered the hospital for another of those sessions, Rennie was there, too, if only in spirit. She endured the pain, the enforced stillness that followed, the long wait until the bandages were removed, the uncertainties and doubts just as surely as if she had been Magda herself.

The worry, the pity, the anxiety, took their toll, and Rennie's own health, at those times, suffered in consequence. She became thin and tense and snappy, and the photographers complained. Little did they guess how Rennie despised them for their lack of sympathy! Little did they guess that she would willingly have borne the pain and waiting herself, suffered those fine-seamed scars on her own smooth olive skin, if only she could have changed places with Magda.

Instead, she posed automatically, aloof and disdainful, imperious and aristocratic, her eyes darkening defiantly as she swept them with a challenging glare, so that they called out admiringly, 'That's *it*, Renata – mag-*nificent*! Just *hold* it!' and Rennie, withdrawn into her own private world of agonizing, held it effortlessly, because she scarcely heard them.

She had been personally responsible for Magda for two years now, although it was actually three since her father had taken his little great-niece into his home after the accident which had been fatal to the child's parents, leaving her entirely alone except for two unfamiliar relations – himself and Rennie. It was typical of his generosity and moral fibre that he had acted as he did, forfeiting the peace and privacy which, as an elderly intellectual, he cherished, and imperilling his relationship with Enid, which was even then none too harmonious.

It came as no surprise to Rennie that Enid had spoken

in the manner in which she had, after the Professor's death.

'We can put the child into a home, Renata. It will be the best place for her, after all. It's impossible to support both myself and her on my annuity.' Enid had sighed. 'So typical of your father, that. He lost an enormous amount of capital on those investments of his, simply because he neglected to keep an eye on them.'

'He didn't neglect, Enid. He just forgot,' Rennie had corrected her quietly, still raw with grief, and unable to hear such a criticism and remain silent.

'*Forgot?*' Enid snorted. 'That's no excuse. One can't afford to forget, where money is concerned! In a way, I'm to blame, though, I suppose. I should have recognized him for the impossible dreamer that he was, and kept my eye on them myself.' A sigh. 'Anyway, it's too late now to have regrets. Inquests are useless, and it's the present that concerns me, not the past. I shall arrange for Magda to go to one of those places for homeless children. I certainly can't afford to keep her.'

'But *I* can,' returned Rennie firmly.

'You?' Enid had regarded her curiously. 'Where, might I ask?'

'At – at the flat.'

'Won't your flat-mate– what's her name? Vivien? – won't she have something to say about that?'

'Oh, Viv won't mind,' avowed Rennie warmly. 'We – I can't just turn her out into the cold, as you suggest.'

'Implying that I can?' Enid's shoulders lifted. 'It's a question of economics, pure and simple, Renata. I can't have her, but if you feel up to trying, you're more than welcome. You're obviously well remunerated in that glamorous job of yours.'

'And started contributing something for Magda's maintenance as soon as I was able,' Rennie felt bound to point out.

'Oh, I'm not saying that you haven't been a suitably dutiful daughter, my dear. The famous Bentmore conscience. Your father had it too.' Enid smiled mirthlessly. 'Well, I'm no Bentmore. I missed out on it, thank God. I always think an overdeveloped sense of obligation is apt to cloud the real issues and cause untold complications, so I'm fortunate not to have been blessed with one! The child isn't my concern, Renata. She isn't now, and never was. But if you choose to make her *yours*, by all means do.'

'Yes, I'll take her. I'll come for her things at the week-end.'

'I'll have them packed and ready.' Enid smiled coolly, although this time with genuine pleasure, it seemed. 'Well, well, Renata. You're quite full of surprises, aren't you? Who'd have guessed at a maternal streak under that gilded exterior! Of course, it may not last for long.'

'For as long as Magda needs me,' returned Rennie tightly, and found her fingers digging painfully into her palms in an all-out effort at self-restraint. It was hardly worth arguing with Enid over this particular problem, although she was already beginning to ask herself if she hadn't been unwisely impulsive.

'What will you do with her in the daytime, while you are at work?' asked Enid now, as though sensing the other's sudden uncertainty.

'There are nursery schools, and things like that. I'll work something out. And Magda will soon be five, and able to attend a proper school full-time.'

But of course, in the end, Magda hadn't been able to do that at all – or at least, far from full-time.

She had instead spent months on end in hospital wards, undergoing a series of plastic operations to repair the damage caused by that shattered windscreen, and she had also had to pass several brief periods in the very establishments which Rennie had intended to avoid – those homes for the homeless.

Rennie felt the familiar blanket of guilt settling over her. She regarded it as an admission of partial failure on her part that she had found it necessary to put Magda into a children's home each time she went abroad on a modelling assignment, and yet what else could she have done? Vivien was working, too, and had her own life to lead, and even if Rennie had not already completely lost touch with her stepmother, she was sure Enid would have refused to take the little girl back, even for a month at a time.

During the first year of her guardianship of Magda, Rennie had been sent to Jamaica, and last time it had been to the Algarve, where she had perched upon hot dry rocks – tanned and agile, lissom as a young animal in a series of bikinis and catsuits – yet unable to enjoy the perfumed air and warmth and sun because of that gnawing anxiety for Magda.

This year – in just three months' time, in fact – she was to go to the ancient city of Fez to do a stint on spring fashions.

Rennie would have found the idea of escaping from the first cool finger-touch of a London winter undeniably attractive, had it not been for the memory of little Magda's widening blue eyes appealing to her through the windows of the institution where she had left her the last time.

As the other inmates roughed and tumbled in the background, ignoring the frail figure of the latest newcomer as she pressed her nose against the glass and made a final, mute entreaty, Rennie had departed swiftly, willing herself not to turn and wave, because she knew that if she did that, there was a distinct possibility that she wouldn't be able to leave Magda there at all.

Now, Morocco beckoned, and so did Magda – but in different directions.

Rennie could feel the spell of the *medina* already – the perfume of the spice-scented souks, the mystery of veiled figures and sandalled feet, the fascination of mosque and dome and minaret, all lured her tantalizingly. The ancient ramparts, the linking gardens of those twin historic, sun-drenched towns urged her to go – and Magda's pleading blue eyes begged her to stay.

Rennie uncrossed her legs from their cramped position in the crowded bus, and surveyed her spattered tights fretfully.

It was only for three weeks this time, wasn't it? So why should she torture herself in this way? She worked hard, she deserved a change of scene for that work, and by and large she had succeeded in looking after Magda fairly well. It hadn't been too easy to maintain the two of them on what had initially seemed an adequate enough income for one, and there had certainly been difficulties about leaving and collecting the child at school, but on the whole Rennie hadn't made too bad a job of being a proxy parent, had she?

She was only feeling like this, now, because she had just left Magda sitting up forlornly with that ridiculous panda in the children's ward, a place that inevitably had a curiously depressing effect upon Rennie – although any certified nursing sister could have told her that it was a far from depressing place to be! It was just the small, pale face, the bandages, the evenings, the *rain*, which were causing Rennie her present pangs and doubts.

Or was it?

Surely she wasn't going to let that unexpected message from Australia go on chipping away at her peace of mind, as it had threatened to do ever since she had received it?

No, she *wasn't*! After all, hadn't she already decided to ignore it, to put it right out of her thoughts? And yet—

Supposing that she was actually *depriving* Magda in some way by her decision?

Rennie pressed the bell at her approaching stop, helped an elderly woman to descend to the lower platform and followed her off the bus, her mind still preoccupied.

She knew every word of that peremptory cable which had arrived out of the blue six weeks ago. It had been a lengthy, reply-paid one, as if the sender grudged the time to write a proper letter, and the teletyped wording had imprinted itself upon Rennie's mind with an indelibility that persisted and annoyed.

The address was presumably a telegraphic one, for it simply said 'Kattelko, Sydney.'

After that, it went on:

'Upon investigation disturbed discover niece Magda Sandasen in neglected circumstances stop Why was I not informed stop Propose take child stop Prepared arrange legal adoption if necessary stop Request you send her out to Sydney earliest opportunity at my expense stop Chalford Sandasen.'

Rennie could still recollect quite vividly her own blank astonishment as she had perused this missive for the first time.

'Read that,' she had finally managed to mutter weakly, as she handed it over to Viv. 'It's incredible!'

'Who's Chalford Sandasen?' her flat-mate had asked, after she, too, had read the cable.

'He must be Neil's brother, or he wouldn't call Magda his niece, I suppose.' She shrugged. 'We knew Neil had a family, of course. He mentioned an elder brother occasionally, but he always said they'd disowned him. He was the "black sheep", and proud of it – and yet sometimes I had a feeling that there was a sort of wistfulness hidden away somewhere amongst all that defiance of Neil's. He spoke of them only seldom, though, even to Betty. I gathered that they had more or less cut him off without the proverbial penny. He seemed to enjoy thumbing his nose at them after that.'

'Was he really as wild as your father said, Rennie? I mean, Magda's such a quiet little thing, it's hard to believe.'

'He was brash, more than wild. Unstable, but tremendously likeable. He was younger than Betty, you know, but they were terribly happy together, even though he was never much of a success.' Her throat tightened. 'He was young, and very human, and he just *loved* life, Viv. It seems terrible to think it was cut short so tragically for both of them.' She sighed. 'He'd gone from job to job without ever settling. He tried his hand at all sorts of peculiar things, and he dragged Betty and the baby around from place to place, and sometimes they didn't even know where the next meal was coming from. The insecurity couldn't have been good for them, but love can make up for an awful lot of other shortcomings. He was a wonderfully generous and loving person, quite unlike this brother, it seems.'

'How do you know?' Viv eyed her curiously.

'Oh, from things Neil used to say . You can even tell it from that cable! Bossy and domineering, the sort who enjoys playing God. Send her out, he says, just like that. Who does he think he *is*?'

'What are you going to do?'

'Do? Nothing.'

'Nothing?' Viv managed to appear startled.

'Absolutely, definitely *nothing*. I mean, how could he expect me just to turn her over like that, when he never even bothered with her father, with his very own brother? I don't know a single thing about him, do I, except that he sounds quite beastly and autocratic. Besides, I resent the way he says "neglected circumstances". What right has he to say such a nasty and sweeping thing as that, after I've done the very best I can for Magda?'

'Perhaps because, compared with what he can offer her himself, they appear to be neglected circumstances?' suggested Viv gently. 'You must admit you worry terribly about her, Rennie, and that the situation is anything but ideal. I love her too, you know that, but maybe I can take a more objective view than you. I mean, even now, she'll hardly be discharged from hospital before you'll have to put her back in that place so that you are able to go off to Fez.'

'I know, I know.' Rennie got up and paced about the room in a sudden, irritable burst of energy. 'It's only for a few weeks, though. And after that I can refuse any more overseas assignments. I agree it's bad for Magda to be shoved around from pillar to post. I'll just tell the agency that I'm not prepared to take work outside London after this.'

Vivien shook her head, her eyes softening at her friend's obvious distress.

'You can't go on opting out of things for ever because of Magda, Rennie,' she pointed out hesitantly. 'You've given up enough already, and here you are again, talking of denying yourself professional opportunities that could further your career.'

'Rubbish, Viv. What are a few modelling engagements,

after all?'

'I wasn't referring necessarily to *modelling* engagements, if it's engagements we're talking about, Rennie,' Viv returned dryly.

'To what, then?'

'To the traditional sort, actually. To your one with Keith.'

'Keith?'

Keith! Odd how the mere mention of his name still had the power to hurt her! Viv had sprung it on her so abruptly that Rennie felt momentarily breathless with shock.

'Keith and I were never engaged, Viv. You know that,' she stated tightly, her voice quivering in spite of her effort to control it.

'But you would have been – if it hadn't been for Magda.'

Rennie shook her head.

'All Keith wanted was – was a sophisticated sort of *affair*,' she corrected bleakly. 'And I wasn't prepared to have one.'

'No, Rennie, be honest. It wasn't as simple as that.' Viv's tone was compassionate, but firm. 'That was because of Magda, too, really, wasn't it? Because he wasn't prepared to take on someone else's child at the outset of his own marriage? If it hadn't been for Magda, you'd have a hoop of diamonds on the fourth finger of your left hand, by now, and a wide gold band as well.'

'Love me, love my dog – or rather, my little cousin,' said Rennie hardily, but her voice was strangely husky and her eyes were misted over with unshed tears – tears which she was quite determined would never fall.

'Oh, *Rennie*! Was that how it was? You issued a sort of ultimatum?'

She nodded miserably.

'But so did *he*. Oh, Viv, let's not talk about it. What's the use?'

She couldn't bear to remember Keith, had imagined that she had been successful in relegating him to the past.

He had been the one great experience of her life, Rennie admitted bitterly. He had taught her all she knew about love, in fact – that it could be rapturous, fleeting, absorbing, fickle. Too fickle, too shallow, too ephemeral to survive the presence of a little orphan-girl appendage with sober appeal in her gaze and thin scars on her cheeks and a worn-looking panda bear in her small, quietly hopeful hands.

Rennie had had lukewarm relationships with several men since then, but, after Keith, she found them lacking in some indefinable way. There was no magic, no spark, no *chemistry*. Or perhaps the fault lay with Rennie herself. Maybe she was a different person now, because she had allowed herself to be so deeply hurt. There was a certain comfort in being numb and cold and unresponsive. If you didn't care, then you didn't suffer. It was as simple as that. If you didn't allow yourself to *care*, you were *safe*!

She ran lightly up the steps of the tall cream building in the Regency terrace where she and Vivien had their apartment, and buzzed for the lift.

At the top floor, she emerged, shut the grille automatically, and fished in her handbag for her key.

Her fingers were still scrabbling when the door opened.

'Oh, Viv, thanks. You're early, surely?'

'And you're late. How was she?'

'Magda?' Rennie unfastened her raincoat, slipped it off and placed it on a hanger in the hall. 'So-so. A bit quiet, I thought, poor mite. Sort of depressed. Or maybe I was and it rubbed off, although I certainly tried to be at my brightest.'

Vivien gave her an odd glance.

'Well, you'll need to *keep* trying, Rennie, I'm afraid – to be your brightest, I mean!'

Something in her tone made the other girl pause in her actions, eyebrows raised questioningly.

'What is it? Not—?' She hesitated. 'Not another cable?'

'You've guessed it in one. They must have tried to

phone it, but we were both out, of course. The envelope was on the floor when I came in. Here.'

Rennie's fingers were shaking unaccountably as she opened it, and read the message. She was silent for so long that her flat-mate finally had to prompt her anxiously.

'Well, Rennie? What does it say?'

'Read it. Read it out aloud, please, Viv, just so that I'm sure I've got it right, will you.'

Viv obliged.

'Kindly despatch Magda Sandasen at earliest convenience stop Consign to Mascot airport Sydney stop Advise ETD and flight number stop Finance available in my name London Branch Kattelko upon identification.' Viv paused. 'That's all. Except for the signature.'

'Chalford Sandasen again. How I'm beginning to loathe that name!'

'What are you going to do this time?'

Viv's voice was concerned. One couldn't but be aware of the glitter of anger in Rennie's lovely brown eyes, the dangerous flush of those high-boned cheeks, the brittle gruffness in her usually tranquil tones.

'I'm going to send him an answer right back, right now.' She marched to the telephone. 'May I have it, Viv? Is it reply-paid again?'

'It is.'

Rennie's teeth flashed in amusement at her companion's gesture of resignation as she returned the cablegram to its rightful owner.

'Don't worry — I know how to deal with *his* sort,' she assured her friend scathingly, as she gave her number, and then she was dictating her reply with measured confidence.

'To Chalford Sandasen, Kattelko, Sydney. This is a human being we are discussing not a pound of sausages stop Refuse dispatch pending further information regarding character and personal credentials. Renata Bentmore.'

'*That* should fix him!' said Rennie with some relish, as she replaced the receiver.

Only, of course it didn't, although for a full week

afterwards Rennie was under the impression that she had silenced that subtle persecutor from the furthest Antipodes, whose suggestions had recently caused her so much soul-searching and loss of sleep.

The next communication was in the form of an air-mailed letter, and it wasn't from Chalford Sandasen at all.

It was from a firm of solicitors – *his* solicitors – and one only had to note the impressive number of additional qualifications after the partners' names, feel the pleasingly substantial texture of the watermarked notepaper, to sense that they were a firm of eminent respectability.

'Dear Madam,' they began with traditional and satisfying deference, 'We have been instructed by our client, Mr. Chalford Sandasen, to communicate with you on his behalf regarding his proposal for the legal adoption of his niece, Miss Magda Sandasen, who is at present, we understand, under your voluntary guardianship. As Mr. Sandasen is a figure of impeccable standing and having substantial interests in the Australian pastoral industry, including Barrindilloo Pastoral Company, Mawsby Investments, Koontilla Pty., and Emu International, together with extensive lesser interests, and as the child Magda Sandasen is legally already his niece, Mr. Sandasen considers that he is suitably placed to give her the best possible opportunities in life. He has instructed us to emphasize the precarious nature of your own occupation as a fashion model; the inexperience of life inevitable in a single woman of a mere twenty-three years and her attendant shortcomings as a permanent guardian; the vagaries of London's climate, with possibly injurious effects upon the health of an unfortunate child, who is evidently unable to share your own frequent excursions to sunnier climes; the lack of financial stability and continuity of schooling. Our client is confident that, upon consideration of all the above-mentioned aspects, you will concur with his wishes in the matter, thus obviating the painful necessity of further legal procedures against you on his part. In this we share our client's optimism, and trust that your good sense will prevail in this matter. May we add, Madam, in the anticipation of further correspondence, that it is most inadvisable to question Mr. Chalford Sandasen's financial, moral or social status. He was, not unnaturally, greatly displeased at the implications of such a query, and we would suggest in all humility that henceforth it would be prudent to resist an impulse possibly engendered by both distance and ignorance. We remain, Madam, your most humble and obedient servants.'

The letter was promptly reinforced by the arrival of yet another cable.

It was brief and to the point.

'Final offer to receive child into my household stop Am prepared finance your chaperonage on trip plus sojourn of three months to accustom Magda to altered circumstances stop Option closes midnight tomorrow Australian time stop Remember we are ten hours ahead. Chalford Sandasen.'

Rennie sank on to the sofa, momentarily stunned.

'Ten hours ahead! Why, that means I have to make up my mind right away!'

She gazed in perplexity from the message still held limply between her slender fingers to her flat-mate, who was already in the act of pouring them both a reviving cup of coffee.

'Viv, for the first time in my life, I just don't know what to do,' she confessed miserably.

'It's quite a decision to make, Rennie, I agree – one that you could tear yourself apart over, in fact.'

'He sounds such a – a brute. And as for those lawyers, they're not *my* humble and obedient servants, whatever they avow at the end of that horrible letter – they're *his*! The entire document reveals his nasty mind at the back of it, all the way through. Precarious nature of your livelihood, he says. Huh!' She gulped a mouthful of coffee indignantly, found it too hot, and replaced the cup hastily back upon its saucer. 'And, Viv, what can he possibly mean by that bit about Magda being unable to accompany me on my excursions to sunnier climes? Do you suppose he has actually found out about the – the children's homes?'

'It certainly looks that way,' admitted Viv reluctantly. 'Remember his very first message began "Upon investigation".'

'A private detective, maybe?' Rennie's voice held disgust. 'But that's *snooping*! It's despicable! And that nasty crack about sunnier climes – you'd think I'd gone off on a holiday each time, instead of those hours and hours of dreary posing, changing, posing, until I could have screamed with boredom and ended up aching in every muscle. It – it's downright *unjust*!'

Vivien shrugged.

'Life is, though, isn't it, at times? I mean, look at poor little Magda herself, the innocent victim of that awful crash. When one thinks of what she has been through in the hospital, too, it seems unfair that it's all had to happen to just one small girl.'

There was utter silence in the flat following this remark.

Rennie sat hunched and preoccupied, staring miserably at the small gas fire that glowed from the wall near her legs, while the other girl finished her own coffee and began quietly to replace the cups on the tray beside her.

It was Vivien who spoke again – haltingly, with a gentle, half-apologetic glance at the dejected figure of the slender model-girl at her side. Even at her most despondent there was a beauty and individuality about Rennie that at this particular moment moved Viv to pity. Her very loveliness made her appear more vulnerable, somehow.

'Rennie darling, I don't want to sway you one way or the other, or interfere, you know that, but well – all that *sunshine*! I mean, just think of it. The sun, the sea, those lovely beaches for a child to romp and play on – Sydney's supposed to have dozens of them, right up the coastline; no money worries, and very probably some other children as playmates, too. He did say he wanted to receive her into his household, didn't he, and that indicates a wife and a family.'

'You think I should let her go?'

'I'm only trying to point out that it does seem like a chance in a million for Magda. An opportunity that may never come her way again. And he *is* her closest relative. I fully believe what his solicitors hint, too, in their letter – that he'll stop at nothing to get her.'

Rennie sighed. There was resignation and defeat in that sound.

'You're right, of course. I've known it myself, all the time, I think. I just didn't want to part with her, I guess. She has become my *raison d'être*, somehow, Viv – a part of my life.'

'Or an excuse for opting out of it? Forgive me, Rennie,' her friend added hastily, seeing the wounded look in the beautiful tawny eyes, 'but you've made Magda the reason for not meeting other men, ever since Keith. Oh, yes, you have! And you can't go on opting out for ever, you know. Come to that, I've always felt that you and he might still—'

'*Do* let's leave it!' begged Rennie, the old anguish flooding through her. 'At least I shall be able to go out with Magda, and see for myself that she is really going to be happy,' she continued brightly, determinedly forcing her mind away from the painful topic of Keith Stamford. 'It's something to be thankful for, that – that I'll be able to see her new home for myself.'

'And quite generous of *him*, too. I mean, think of it, three months on that sunny southern continent! I'm beginning to envy you, Rennie!'

The other girl spread her fingers in a disparaging gesture.

'Generosity is relative to one's means,' she pointed out tersely. 'I dare say, from what those solicitors said in their letter, that my return fare from England is just a tiny drop in the ocean to their precious client. It'll mean no more to him than a ticket on the tube from Piccadilly to Oxford Circus! And he'll be *there*, won't he, Viv, for the whole of my sunny three months? In all his autocratic splendour? So I don't think you need envy me too much. I detest his very name! I shall hate every minute of it!' she declared with uncharacteristic vehemence.

Viv pursed her lips and wisely changed course.

'What about Morocco, Rennie? Will you still go? And when do you plan to leave with Magda?'

'As soon as she's discharged, I expect. She'll be able to have the necessary vaccination in hospital, I'm sure, if I have a word with the Sister. There's no point in waiting longer, and it would hardly be worth her while starting school again here, for such a short time. As for Fez—' she shrugged fatalistically – 'I shall have to cancel it, that's certain. I don't suppose they'll ever ask me again, they'll be so fed up. Ah, well, it's all one can expect, in my particular livelihood – it's so competitive, and there's always someone just waiting to take one's place, and step right into one's shoes, and oust one from the lists. Maybe that's the *precarious* bit that that odious man referred to!' There was a bite in her voice, because she was endeavouring to hide her very real disappointment.

It was for Magda's sake, though, she reminded herself grimly, and she had done so much for the little girl, ungrudgingly, already, that she must try to make this final gesture in as warm-hearted a manner as possible.

Poor dear little Magda! It wasn't *her* fault, after all!

Rennie went to the telephone, and sent the reply that was obviously expected of her, and when she put down the instrument it was with a sense of finality, irrevocability. And foreboding? Surely not! What was there to feel apprehensive about, after all? As Viv had rightly said, it was a chance in a million for the child, and for herself it meant a mere three months' leave of absence. She would soon pick up the threads again when she returned, even if some competitor had jostled her out of her position at the top.

She became absorbed in the problem of how best to broach the topic to Magda.

It would need to sound like an exciting and enjoyable adventure, a marvellous excursion to a magical land, to a mystery-place, a continent seamed with antiquity, where barren ranges erupted out of limitless plains, and slow-moving rivers writhed tortuously into billabongs as they lazed, groping their way to soak finally away into the depths of the earth itself, and strange marsupials – the oddities of the nature world – bounded through endless scrub, and magnetic anthills stood high and desolate – sequestered graveyards paying homage to the north – and the pallid trunks of ghost-gums rose like lonely sentinels against the ochre of crumbling red ridges. A land of a thousand horizons, of shimmering sunsets and blazing dawns, of aborigines and boomerangs and kangaroos and swagmen – of all the things, indeed, that Rennie, and others like her, had gathered from those inviting travel posters and documentaries that one sees from time to time, luring the reader and the viewer to that other, distant hemisphere.

Rennie didn't want to be lured. She was happy enough where she was.

But Magda was different. For Magda she must be glad, must use her eloquence in an effort to enthral the little girl with all the exciting possibilities that the posters kept proclaiming. It shouldn't be too difficult. And then there would be passports, inoculations, tickets, packing, good-byes.

Rennie's mind was still grappling with details as she got ready for bed that night. When she drew the blankets up, she also seemed to enshroud herself in a vague unhappiness, a dejection of spirit, a feeling too blurred and uncertain to allow definition, yet one that prevented her from falling asleep as the weary hours of the night ticked past.

Finally, when it was almost dawn, she drifted into uneasy slumber, and the dreams from which she could not rouse tormented and taunted her. They were of Keith, so near, so exquisitely near that she could have reached out and touched him. And then a voice was calling her away – a child's voice – Magda's high treble, full of desperate appeal. And just as she was kneeling down to gather the little girl into her arms to comfort her, there was quite suddenly no child there at all – just an envelope lying on the ground where Magda had been. A message that said 'Option closes midnight tomorrow' – and Rennie woke in a panic, pale and unrefreshed, to the realization that Chalford Sandasen had had the last word, even in her dream, and that she herself had no further choice in the matter, after all!

CHAPTER TWO

THE last days of October were crisply cold, with that still, pale sunshine and cloud-free sky that Rennie loved, and which were apt to make one forget that winter was just around the corner.

There had been a delay in Magda's discharge from hospital, and the specialist had wished to see her again a fortnight later, but even so, Rennie found that she was hardly prepared for their departure when the day arrived. There had been so many things to which to attend, because, although she herself could only expect to be absent from Britain for a few months, at the most, Magda would be leaving England for good. For *ever*!

The thought chilled Rennie.

What would she do, once her responsibility and preoccupation with the little girl were so abruptly withdrawn? She loved the child, had made her the focal point of her own life over the past eighteen months – ever since Keith had gone out of it, in fact! Perhaps Viv was justified in what she had said, up to a point. Maybe Rennie *had* permitted Magda to gain too secure a hold upon her heart. Once this unique, absorbing interest was removed, she was beginning to ask herself bleakly what she would do instead.

She had been unable to resist spending lavishly upon Magda for her journey to her new home. Perhaps because of a subconscious wish to make up to the child for those angry scars upon her pale little cheeks, Rennie had indulged in an impulsive spending spree, and as a result, Magda was now the possessor of two air-weight cases full of exciting and pretty clothes.

Rennie had thought of everything – dresses, both party and plain; skirts, tunics, and blouses: a neat little trouser suit, for best, and pretty sleeping wear; even a tiny kilt, with a matching Shetland jersey in the same periwinkle blue colour as Magda's eyes.

Just as well that Chalford Sandasen was paying for their fares, she thought ruefully, as she helped Magda to fasten her buttons and slipped a smart blue pinafore over the child's head.

'That's right, darling. How sweet you look! And we can change the top during our journey. I've got some spare shirts in this little hold-all, you see, so that we can both feel and look fresh when we reach Sydney. Now, put on your shoes, and you'll be ready. I shan't be a moment myself. The taxi will be here in just five more minutes.'

Rennie had done her own packing haphazardly. Her wardrobe was a sophisticated, professional one, and she had plucked a few of her favourite outfits from their hangers and placed them on top of her frilly, feminine underwear and night attire, crammed a silk kimono into a corner, and closed the lid of her solitary suitcase. That should be adequate for all the time she would be staying. Life between one big city and another was much the same, and what was suitable for London would no doubt do in Sydney too.

For the plane trip, she had chosen a simple jersey blazer-suit in toast-brown and white. It was virtually uncrushable, completely classic, and she could vary her choice of blouses from light-weight wool to coolest cotton, as she had planned to do with Magda.

Hatless, she gave her image a final critical inspection, picked up her tan pigskin bag, and with a last careful look around the room, followed Viv and Magda to the lift.

Viv was the only person to see them off.

She stood at the barrier, loyal and encouraging and bright to the very last moment, when they gave that rather forlorn wave from the other side of the Emigration barrier, and made for the departure gate.

Magda was flushed with excitement.

She slept for only a short while on the first stage of the flight, and pressed her face enthusiastically to the window when Bermuda's green-fringed islands, with their pink sandy bays and bobbing white yachts, strung themselves out in the mottled emerald sea below. They went into the airport buildings, drank lemonade, posted a card to Viv.

Magda's eyes were round with wonder as she surveyed the vivid scenes that surrounded her. Never before had she seen such depth of colour in the flowers that spilled in abundance over short, clipped lawns. Never before had she stood beneath such a stark, cloudless brightness, where fluttering flags made gaudy splashes as they waved against the blue sky. She stared with open curiosity at the helmeted policemen in their neat khaki shorts, at the stirring palms and gaily clad groups of people standing on the airport terrace watching as the plane was refuelled, and the laughing band of dark-skinned women who had been tidying the aircraft's interior came giggling down the stairway again.

Shortly after that, the boarding call came once more.

At Nassau they climbed out again, glad of the opportunity to stretch their legs. By the time the plane neared Mexico, darkness had fallen, and Magda was sound asleep. Rennie leaned over her and looked down through the window into the night.

A fairyland of tiny lights winked up from the earth – a delicate tracery of golden lace, it seemed, so fragile and beautiful as to be unbelievable. They then lost height, and the lace resolved itself into wide, parallel streets and ordered squares. Mexico City – that remarkable city of the high plains – sprawled on its plateau some seven thousand feet above the sea, displayed in that nocturnal panorama all the mathematical precision of layout with which Cortez had rebuilt the plundered Indian civilization of some two thousand years before.

Rennie marvelled.

It was difficult to embrace the thought of thousands of years of continuous existence – and yet she had to try, for wasn't she on her way to a land which was as old as time itself? 'The land of living fossils', Australia was sometimes called, with its strange mammals and marsupials clinging to the remnants of their prehistoric tails in a manner unknown anywhere else on earth, and its black-skinned inhabitants still wandering in the deepest interior in a nomadic search for daily food, fashioning their bark water-carriers, their coolamons, making the woomeras to

27

couch their spears, and sharpening their stone axes with a skill that had been preserved and inherited down the centuries from the Age of Stone itself.

Rennie sighed.

In different circumstances, she might have found herself looking forward to this trip! As it was, the feelings of uncertainty and unhappiness and apprehension for Magda were still uppermost in her mind.

What if Chalford Sandasen turned out to be even worse than his ogre image? What if his wife didn't *want* another child in the household? (He didn't sound the type who'd have consulted her, anyway, but Rennie had only to remember Enid to realize that there were a hundred subtle ways in which a woman could make another's child unwelcome!) And what if his own family didn't take to the newcomer? What if—

She stifled this unprofitable line of thought as the jet settled gracefully on to the runway, and lights scudded past the windows. She eased herself over with care to look out, reluctant to disturb the sleeping Magda.

Shortly afterwards, at Acapulco, the child still slept, one hand clutching the disreputable panda.

'I'll keep an eye on her if you'd like to go into the building.'

'Would you? Thanks.' Rennie gave the steward a grateful smile, and got up stiffly.

It was a long, long distance to that shadowy mystery-continent, and they were not even half-way there yet!

It was at Papeete, at five o'clock in the morning, that Keith Stamford walked back into Rennie's life.

Or, to be precise, he walked *ahead* – not back.

Then something made him stop and turn around, and his eyes met Rennie's for a split second, as men's eyes so often did – and then they returned to her face in a look of half-stunned recognition.

He left the little group of airline personnel with whom he had been walking and talking, and came back, over the dark expanse of tarmac, to her side.

'Rennie! I can't believe it!'

'Hullo, Keith.' She smiled tremulously.

He was a Captain now, a four-striper. In the well-cut, dark uniform, the braided cap, he was as debonair and dashing as she remembered.

She felt light-headed with shock.

'You aren't with K.L.M. any more?' What a prosaic question, when her heart was almost suffocating her with its hurried beating, and her limbs felt as if they had been turned to jelly!

'Does it look like it?' The old smile flashed out, but for all his bantering tone, Keith's eyes were lingering. Something of the familiar, male possessiveness lurked in their dark depths as they held her in a strangely fascinating gaze. 'No, I switched lines, and in due course promotion followed. The devil takes care of his own, you know! But you? Are you boarding just now?'

She nodded.

'Magda's in the aircraft, too. I'm taking her to her new guardian in Sydney.'

Keith's gaze was still locked with her own, but there was an instant, subtle sharpening of his expression.

'To Sydney? Do you mean – for *good*?'

'On Magda's part, yes, for good,' Rennie agreed somewhat bleakly, and explained quickly what had happened.

'I see.' Keith glanced at his watch impatiently. 'Damn it all, Rennie, I'll have to go, and so will you.'

'Yes, I know. Goodbye, Keith. It was fun to run into you.'

'Fun, *hell*! Is that all you have to say? Listen to me, Rennie—' his voice was hurried, urgent, as he thought fast – 'Where are you staying in Sydney?'

'I don't know.'

'Then wait for me at the airport, do you hear? Don't leave the building till I've seen you again. You're not going to walk into my life and out of it again, just like that, whatever you think. I'm on this run for another few months, Tahiti to Sydney. I've a couple of days' leave coming to me just now, and I get it fairly regularly, so don't you dare walk out of Mascot until we arrange something.'

'But I—'

'But nothing. *Will* you, Rennie? *Promise?*'

He was looking down at her in that old, endearing, cajoling way, and Rennie felt herself weakening. For all her resolution not to become involved again, there was no doubt that Keith still had that old magical power over her. He had always been aware of the fact, and had never hesitated to use his charms ruthlessly as and when the need arose. He had been perplexed and hurt when Rennie had refused to have an affair with him, that she knew. Keith was accustomed to getting his own way where women were concerned — even beautiful, independent women such as Renata Bentmore — and he had been entirely unable to understand Rennie's attitude.

It had all hinged on the child, though — on Magda Sandasen, who was even now fast asleep in the big jet airliner that Keith was taking on its final hop to Sydney, and who was soon to be handed over to another guardian — *permanently.*

When he smiled at her, caressingly, like that, Rennie found herself quite unable to do more than smile weakly back, and mutter an indistinct and somewhat breathless assurance that she would speak to him again at their destination.

Satisfied, he strode off to rejoin the group who were by now entering the plane's forward section, and Rennie herself walked blindly up the passenger gangway.

The remainder of the journey passed in a daze.

They touched down at Nadi in the Fijis — 'the last duty-free call', the steward reminded them, and Rennie bought a small flask of French cologne and a few cigarettes, which was all that her meagre purse would allow, although she had wisely set aside a more generous sum for emergencies. She did not smoke herself, but supposed that these items might be acceptable and unembarrassing gifts for her host and hostess, when she and Magda finally met them.

Approaching Sydney, the flight route took them over the coast, and there — scarcely any way down, it seemed, and clearly visible in bright sunshine — were the wonderful beaches of which Viv had spoken so enviously. They stretched for miles both ways, like a scalloped border against the coastal scrubland – the sand so clean and white, the frothing surf gnawing tirelessly at its pale edges. These were the very beaches where Magda would soon be playing, probably in the company of Chalford Sandasen's own children. Soon her limbs would become strong and brown, and the sea breezes would whip colour into her pallid cheeks, and gradually the thin, livid scars would recede and Magda would become a gay, laughing, energetic, *pretty* little girl – a little 'new' Australian.

Rennie gazed down in awe, feeling somehow slightly happier about the whole thing. The glaring sun and sparkling sea and inviting sands were telling her that she had done the right thing in allowing Magda to come, after all. If Rennie had to part with her, at least it was to a better, healthier, and more exciting way of life. One could hardly argue with such bounties of nature as those!

And then they were wafting down for the final halt at Kingsford Smith airport, and for the last time Rennie was bracing herself against the seat and smiling reassurance at her little companion through the rush of noise as the brakes were applied, and the giant jet came to rest and then began to taxi to its disembarkation point.

They were here! Rennie felt weary but triumphant now that the journey – an entire half-world's flight – was over.

She claimed their luggage, went through Customs, and out into the milling throng at the bustling terminal. She had just spied Keith when a call came over the speaker, and Rennie heard her own name called.

'Would Miss Renata Bentmore please report to the Information Desk. Miss Renata Bentmore, to Information. Thank you.'

'Over here. I'll come with you.' Keith put a guiding hand beneath her elbow, and steered her through the crowd, while Magda waited obediently beside the cases.

At Information, a man came forward and raised his hat.

31

'Miss Bentmore? Krantz is my name. I've come from Mawsby Investments on Mr. Sandasen's instructions, to meet you and your – er – cousin, is it? – and to take you to your hotel.'

'Hotel!' Rennie took his extended hand, shook it politely, and collected herself. 'But I thought we would be going to Mr. Chalford Sandasen's own home. Does he *live* in a hotel, perhaps?'

The man, middle-aged, unremarkable in a pepper-and-salt worsted suit, gave her an odd look.

'Chad? Good lord, no! He's out of town just now, though, and reckoned he probably couldn't make it, so he asked me to deputize for him. I'm to take you to the Eucalypt Grove, where you'll be quite comfortable for the night. Or maybe *two* nights. In any case, you're to remain there till Chad gets in touch himself.'

'I see. Thank you, then, Mr. Krantz.' She indicated her baggage, upon which Magda was patiently sitting, and followed the man from Mawsby Investments.

'It's perfect,' murmured Keith in her ear. 'I'll be round tonight, Rennie. I know the Eucalypt Grove, of course – it's very central.' He smiled in that disturbing way. 'We'll go out on the town.'

'Tonight? Oh, Keith, I *can't*. How could I, with Magda and everything?' Rennie felt torn between common sense and longing – the old yearning that his proximity could awaken so easily still, it appeared.

'Of course you can! The Eucalypt Grove doubtless runs a child-minding service – places of that standard always do. Presumably you've brought some of the famous Renata Bentmore haute couture along? Good! Dress up for me, Rennie, and I'll dig out my dinner jacket. We'll paint the city red!' He bent his head and kissed her, fleetingly but deliberately. 'It will be like old times,' he promised in a murmur. And then he was shouldering his way back through the people, and Rennie herself was following the porter and Magda and the unremarkable Mr. Krantz to the exit.

There was a strange singing in her head, and her feet suddenly seemed to have grown wings.

Soon they were nudging through the heavy traffic in Mr. Krantz's comfortable car. To Rennie the drivers appeared to lack the discipline and orderliness of London's controlled lanes of vehicles. Once or twice she found herself catching her breath as a brightly coloured cab shot inconsiderately across their bows, and several times other drivers gestured angrily as an unruffled Mr. Krantz made a swift and probably lawless dash into a position they already obviously coveted for themselves. He appeared not a whit perturbed, and Rennie eyed his profile with increasing respect after that.

'What do you do, in Mawsby Investments?' she asked politely, during a lull at a traffic light.

'Accounts, mostly. Why?'

'I just wondered. You referred to Mr. Chalford Sand-asen as Chad. I thought you might perhaps be a relation, or a – a director?'

He grinned.

'It's a nice compliment, Miss Bentmore, but no, all the same. The Accounts Department keeps me quite busy enough without a directorship thrown in, and I'm glad to have Chad as my boss, to look after more general policy. I suppose you think it strange that I call him that? Well, it's simple, really – everybody does.'

'Everybody?'

'*Everybody*. He's at the top of the pyramid, of course, and we've the greatest respect and affection for him, so don't be misled. Chad is just another name for Boss, you know, with *us*. It's not a familiarity, so to speak.' He shrugged half-apologetically. 'You'll see what I mean in time. No doubt you will be calling him Chad yourself soon.'

'I?'

'You. Same as the rest of us. Like I said, everybody does, and everybody includes you too, doesn't it, eh?'

He swung the car into a wide circular driveway, and pulled up beside a sky-high white building. It had extensive lawns, tennis courts, a swimming pool, a nine-hole golf course, and a vastly-windowed convex front.

Rennie could scarcely do more than gaze at these fabulous precincts.

'It's a beautiful hotel, isn't it? It reminds me of the Bahamas.'

'Not a hotel, a *motel*. Don't you have them much in England? Like America, Australia's got her share.' He came around and opened her door. 'I think you'll be quite comfortable. Chad said just to go ahead and order anything you like for yourself or the kid. He also suggested that you might like to rest this afternoon, and have an early night. You're quite free to explore the city, of course, if you feel up to it.'

'Thank you. And thank you, too, for meeting us, Mr. Krantz.'

'Don't mention it. 'Bye, then, Miss Bentmore.'

'Goodbye.'

Their rooms were near the top, with a magnificent view. They consisted of a bedroom with twin divans, a tiny bathroom, a spacious sitting-room and a small entrance vestibule with a built-in coat-stand and hat-rack.

The floor above was taken up with restaurants, snack and cocktail bars, hairdressing salons, and an open-air viewing terrace. At ground level, Rennie found a breakfast-room which also served light midday meals. After lunch and some excited exploration on Magda's part, they both had a sleep, and then went out for a walk in the spacious grounds.

Later, Rennie showered and washed her hair in preparation for her evening with Keith. She had had no difficulty in hiring a sitter to keep an eye on Magda in her absence, in case the little girl should wake up and find herself in a strange room and become frightened. Rennie had both explained to the child and met the person who would be on duty, a kind, quiet woman whose husband was one of the night porters in the building. She had little doubt that Magda would sleep, however, after the long and wearisome flight. She herself was desperately tired, too. Had it not been for Keith, she knew that she would thankfully have gone to bed, but instead she was filled with a delicious and nostalgic anticipation at the thought of an evening to be spent in his company.

She dressed that night with her customary professional care, in a simple, high-necked, long-sleeved dress of emerald silk jersey. It was dramatic in that it was virtually backless, revealing Rennie's slender, honey-tanned shoulder-blades, the faint line of her spine, to a tantalizing point just below the waist. It was utterly correct and yet unquestionably seductive, and Rennie knew instinctively that Keith could not fail to be impressed.

He was!

Darkly handsome in dinner jacket and immaculately knotted black tie, he simply stood in the doorway and stared. Then he came over to where she waited and put his hands up, carefully, one on either side of her face, and ran them down gently, as though she were a fragile Dresden figurine, to rest them finally, lightly, upon her silken-clad shoulders.

'Rennie!' His gaze devoured her soberly. 'I believe I'd forgotten how indescribably lovely you are!'

Forgotten? Ah, Keith. How could he have forgotten so easily, so quickly, so effortlessly, when she had tried so hard to forget *him*, and had failed so miserably? Keith, at his most tactless.

'Shall we go?' He took up her wrap and placed it over her shoulders. 'Is the child asleep?'

'Yes, absolutely sound. She's tired out, poor little sweet.'

Rennie went through from the vestibule where they had been standing, to announce her departure to the sitter.

'Where are we going?' she asked, as they went down in the lift to the ground floor.

'There's a plushy joint I know up at the Cross. We'll make for there.'

King's Cross was obviously to Sydney what Soho was to London, the vital night-heart of the great city, a mixture of theatreland and eating houses, snooker dives and discotheques, a burgeoning complex of international establishments.

Up past the Alamein Fountain, the lights were scintillating and the crowds were jostling. Music thudded from a narrow opening, and dim figures moved behind bamboo blinds. Drivers darted from illegally waiting cars to grab a paper at the all-night magazine stall and scurried back to their vehicles while the cab's meter-clock ticked on. A long-haired youth lounged in a doorway, playing a tin whistle to attract people to the stall which his mini-skirted girl-friend was running. It had leather goods and basketware, and a few cheaper ornaments. The rivals over the road were countering the tin whistle with a badly-played bouzouki – they wore leather clothes themselves, and were superior about their cheap rings and tawdry bangles. A muted glow from a café reflected glass-topped tables inside – a passing glimpse of Chianti bottles and candlelit benches and a fat, black-garbed woman lifting snaky tendrils of pasta from a cauldron right in front of the customers' gaze. Under an awning incense was selling and joss sticks changed hands with ritualistic earnestness. Smouldering peace symbols of the hippie brigade. 'The laugh of your life,' a man yelled suggestively with monotonous regularity as he stood beside a lurid poster and beckoned passers-by invitingly to partake of the hidden thrills awaiting them down a steep wooden stair. In a poorly-lit window a Mexican was busy pounding beans. From inside, the musty smell of frijoles fought with the garlicky onslaught of a pizza-house across the street. A sidewalk artist sketched with speed, crouching beside his dirty chalks and sliding his eyes at the upturned hat that lay a discreet distance away, just far enough to give the public time to realize that they were in the presence of a pavement Picasso. Taxis queued outside the theatres, spilling out their extravagantly elegant cargoes. A delicatessen was doing a roaring trade in Continental sausage, and two inebriates rolled out of a neighbouring wine-bar and whistled at a group of cabaret girls who were about to report for their evening stint at something that called itself the Parrot Place.

It seemed to Rennie that all the world and his wife were there. Italian, French, Spanish, Greek, Japanese, Chinese, Hungarian, Indian – all were there in a chaotic, mingling, seething mass of humanity, from the elite society teenster and the famous entertainer to the scruffiest vagrant, the housewife on a birthday treat.

It was almost incredible, after making her way with Keith through the pulsing throng outside, to find herself suddenly in a peaceful atmosphere of subdued luxury.

Shaded lights played up the elegance of the understated decor; waiters, black-jacketed, perceptive, hovered quietly about the tiny, intimate alcoves, or bore trays aloft amongst the small cluster of central tables. On a recessed platform a man's fingers tinkled over the mellow keys of a baby grand, phrasing nostalgic fragments of popular melodies of the past and present with a discreet softness that did not intrude upon the diners' conversation.

Rennie was ushered to a soft, leather-padded seat and presented with a small but absurdly exotic menu.

Her eyes met her escort's over the tiny oblong of snowy damask that separated them.

'Just like I said, Rennie? Like old times?' Keith suggested softly, and Rennie thought her heart might melt away with the pure, exquisite pain that she experienced at his look.

He gave the waiter her order, then his own, chose a wine, offered her a cigarette.

'No? You still don't smoke?' He took one himself, lit it, inhaled. 'Now tell me, Rennie, what have you been doing these past two years?'

'Oh, this and that.' She brushed aside the heartache, the loneliness, the anguish over little Magda, in a single pat phrase. 'And you, Keith? You didn't marry.'

He raised an amused brow.

'Now, what makes you think that?' At Rennie's startled face, he laughed outright. 'No, I'm only teasing you, Rennie. You are quite right. I didn't marry.'

He drew on the cigarette between his fingers, eyeing her consideringly through the faint haze of smoke.

'I suppose I was subconsciously waiting,' he told her at length, 'for this very moment in time. For the moment, my sweet, when you would walk right back into my existence, free of encumbrances!'

Keith's voice was satirical, almost suave.

It was part of his attraction for Rennie that she never quite knew where she was with him. She, in her turn, had always tried to play the game lightly, to keep him guessing as to the extent of her feelings for him. It was this that had saved her face so admirably at that devastating time when they had had the row over Magda, and parted in consequence.

Rennie's only consolation had been that Keith was not aware of either the depth of her emotions or the capacity he had for inflicting hurt upon her. He could have had no idea how vulnerable she was, and how miserable in the ensuing months. He could have had no idea, either, that something inside Rennie had frozen in self-defence, and had remained numb and cold within her ever since. Nor, she hoped, could he guess that, right now, that something was beginning to thaw at his very proximity, spreading an agreeable warmth right through her being.

She wished that he hadn't added that little bit about encumbrances, just then.

It disappointed her vaguely that Keith had never understood her own viewpoint about Magda, and that he had been unable to accept responsibility for the little orphaned girl, as well as for Rennie, in an open-hearted and generous manner.

Faint signs of tarnish on her shining idol?

Well, maybe. But Rennie realized that there were doubtless many men – and very nice men, at that – who found themselves virtually unable to recognize or love any child but their own. They, too, would have acted in precisely the same way as Keith, she supposed, without regarding themselves as in any way lacking in normally affectionate paternal qualities.

Still, it would have been nice if Keith had been one of the *other* ones. The few. The loving-and-*giving*, rather than the loving-and-*demanding*.

Funny to think that, if Keith had been one of those ones, she would not have had to bring Magda to Australia at all. She would not have had a lengthy telegraphic battle with that tyrannical Chalford Sandasen. She would not have received that outwardly respectful, but subtly scarifying letter from that eminent firm of lawyers. She would not have had to wave forlornly to Viv from the wrong side of Emigration Control, nor sit cramped-up and tense in the rear of a big jet plane, trying to keep an apprehensive little child amused and occupied through a long, wearying journey from one hemisphere to the other.

Instead, she would have been in Fez, posing against a background of mosques and minarets in some elegantly floating spring creation, for the cover of a world-renowned glossy magazine.

She would not have run into Keith at all.

'I've never regarded her as an encumbrance, Keith,' she reminded him rather wistfully.

'No, *you* haven't. I know that, Rennie. It was all on my side, and I'm quite prepared to admit it. I actually admired you for the stand you took, if you want the truth, but I can't say I'm sorry to learn that you'll soon be swinging clear of that particular responsibility, all the same. I can't pretend, and *won't* pretend, that Magda could ever have meant a thing to me, and I certainly wasn't going to share *you* with anyone, even with a child. She's in a bit of mess, isn't she, by the way, with all those scars? D'you think it will have been worth it? I hardly dared to look.' He shrugged. 'That sort of thing rather sickens me, actually. I prefer my physical specimens unblemished – preferably slim and blonde and twenty-three, into the bargain!'

Oddly, Rennie found that she could not smile, although his attempt at levity was obvious.

'The surgeon assured me that the marks will disappear in time. She's so young that there's a very good chance of almost complete recovery, cosmetically speaking. Poor little mite! She's been so good and patient through it all that I only hope he's right!'

Keith ground out his cigarette, got up and came around to her chair.

'Let's forget it all tonight, anyway, Rennie. Let's dance,

shall we?'

She rose obediently, and they made their way amongst the tables to a balcony that opened off the far end of the room, and where an orchestra had already played a couple of numbers.

Held in his arms, Rennie forgot her weariness and the tiny feeling of vexation that had just now been niggling at her, lost in the magic of his nearness.

Keith drew her close, and together they kept time to the music in that classic, almost stationary, 'nightclub' form of dancing which goes with dim lights, too small a floor, and too many people. He put his head down so that his cheek brushed her own, and she was happy just to stay that way, revelling in the moment, unable to prevent a warm tide of emotion from flooding through her.

It was well after midnight when Keith took her back to the Eucalypt Grove, and even then it was at Rennie's own insistence.

'Yes, truly, Keith. I'm beginning to feel quite light-headed. I hadn't counted on an evening out straight after a twelve-thousand-mile non-stop journey, you know. And anyway, I mustn't leave Magda for longer, although I'm sure she'll sleep sounder tonight than ever in her whole life, probably. The sitter will be wondering where I am, too.'

'Nonsense! She's probably fast asleep over her knitting!'

'Even so, I really must go. *Please*.'

'Very well.' He was still reluctant, but he beckoned to the waiter to bring the bill. 'You don't know your plans for the future yet?'

'No. Mr. Krantz said we might be there tomorrow night, too, but we just have to wait until we are contacted, it seems.'

'Hm. I'll call tomorrow, then, on the off-chance. In any case, you have my address and phone number, haven't you, Rennie?'

'They're safely in my bag.' She indicated her small gold brocade evening purse.

'Good. We mustn't lose touch *now*, must we?'

There was something deliciously meaningful in the way in which Keith stressed that 'now'.

Outside, King's Cross had become fully awake, it seemed.

The crowds were even thicker, if that were possible, the noises louder, the cooking smells more pervasive, the lights more scintillating than they had been a few hours earlier. Night-life, in all its brash, bold, brazen gaiety, was in full swing, and would be for hours yet! Even the newspaper stall was still carrying on a buoyant trade, and around the Alamein Fountain there were more people than ever, grouped about, gazing hypnotically at the showering cascade of whispering waters.

The taxi turned down another street, passed a hamburger waggon where a man in a white overall was serving a lengthy queue that varied from men in dinnerjackets and women in theatre dress to bearded hippies and leather-booted lovelies.

'I'll come up with you. Have you got your key?' Back at the motel, Keith pressed the lift button, and they soared up together to the second-top floor.

Rennie turned the key softly, and stepped into the entrance vestibule, turned.

'It's been a wonderful evening, Keith. Marvellous, in fact.'

'I thought so, too. Rennie. We must do it again.'

'Yes, *please*.'

'Tomorrow? I mean, tonight, of course – I'd forgotten it was so long past midnight, and time has a habit of passing too quickly when you're around. Much too quickly.'

She hesitated.

'I'm just not sure quite what we're doing,' she felt bound to remind him. 'But I could let you know.'

'No, I'll phone you. Or better still, I'll look in.' He took her gently into his arms. 'What luck, to meet like that at Papeete! Some instinct must have told me that there was a beautiful damsel following me, and made me turn my head. Just think, if I hadn't looked around when I did, we wouldn't have had this date tonight!'

41

'Oh, Keith! I'm so glad you *did* look around!'

Rennie's voice was husky. She knew that he was going to kiss her, knew just what Keith's kisses could do to her. She had a half-desire to escape, to avoid that soul-searing, earth-shaking emotion that he could arouse in her, yet she could only stand there mutely, caught in the fatal web of attraction that bound her to him, waiting for the exquisite moment when his lips would find hers.

They kissed long and passionately, and it was Rennie, breathless and bewildered, who finally struggled out of Keith's hold.

'God, Rennie, you're a witch!' His voice came thickly. 'If it wasn't for that child, I—'

'Hush, Keith, or you'll wake her. Please go now,' Rennie pleaded.

He gave her a brief, final caress.

'She won't be around much longer, anyway, so I guess I'll have to be patient. Goodnight, my sweet, darling Rennie. You're quite the nicest and most alluring little airport pick-up I've ever had the luck to encounter!' He chuckled. 'Sweet dreams,' he whispered, and then he closed the door gently behind him, and was gone.

Rennie hung her wrap on one of the coat-hooks, turned, gave a gasp of pure fright as a shadowy figure detached itself from the lintel of the inner doorway where it had been lounging.

'Miss Bentmore, I presume?' drawled a deep voice from the gloom, and that same deep voice had a certain, definitely nasty overtone. 'A touching goodnight, I must say. And *you* had the unutterable presumption and audacity to question *my* character!'

With a tiny flutter of complete dismay, Rennie realized in a single, uninspired guess that the owner of that silky, sarcastic drawl could be none other than Mr. Chalford Sandasen himself!

CHAPTER THREE

'Mr. Sandasen?' she exclaimed stupidly. 'I – thought you were out of town!' She put a slender, manicured hand to her throat to still the tiny pulse that fluttered there.

'That much is obvious,' he assured her, with cold disapproval. 'When I instructed Krantz to tell you to order anything you liked, Miss Bentmore, a *baby-sitting* service was a long way from my thoughts, I can assure you! What sort of a girl *are* you? On your very first night in a strange country, to abandon a child and go out with some – some lounge lizard you've bumped into on the way out! If I hadn't heard the whole thing, I'd scarcely be able to believe it! As it was, I sent that woman off to her bed, and remained here myself. You *are* aware of the time, I presume? Or did all other thoughts but those so obviously shared with your companion desert your mind entirely?'

Rennie ran her tongue over her lips. She was dizzy with fatigue and reaction.

Now that Keith had departed, the exhilaration which had kept her going throughout the evening was there no more. The magic had fled, and in its place there was only agonizing embarrassment and this peculiar light-headedness – no doubt brought on by the very real fright she had just received.

She stared at the man, lost for words. He didn't look as though he'd be impressed by anything she had to say, anyway, she realized bleakly, as she took in the imperious mould of the lean, deeply tanned face, too angular to be conventionally handsome, with its high forehead and squared-off jaw. He had mid-brown hair that was almost as bleached in places as the sun-gold, jutting brows which cragged above heavily-lidded eyes of a singularly clear, glittering green colour.

As he stepped out from the doorway, Rennie instinctively noted the excellent cut of the pale grey, lightweight suit he wore, the fashionable double-vented jacket, the perfection of the narrow trousers, and the rightness of that particular tie which lifted the whole effect from the merely immaculate to the unquestionably elegant.

He wore his clothes with the carelessness of the outdoor man who doesn't give a hoot for such things – and indeed, thought Rennie, with that tall, narrow-hipped, athletic frame, obviously in the peak of physical condition, and the almost panther-like grace with which he moved, he didn't *have* a care, did he?

She raised her eyes, met the steady, penetrating gaze of those peculiar, almost phosphorescent green orbs.

'It's not like you think at all, Mr. Sandasen,' she muttered breathlessly, cursing her voice for its momentary indecisiveness, which could almost be mistaken for lack of conviction.

He made an impatient gesture.

'Look, Miss Bentmore' – and the deep, smooth drawl was impatient, now, too – 'if you're thinking of trying to gammon me, I don't advise you to try it!'

'Gammon you?' She looked bewildered.

'Sorry. I forgot you don't yet know the lingo. To gammon is to – er – issue a false statement.' His mouth twisted without humour.

'Why can't you just say "lie", then, and be done with it?' demanded Rennie hotly, with returning spirit. 'And I'm *not* trying to – to gammon you. How dare you even suggest such a thing! I – we – Keith and I – we are – old friends.'

'Yes? How old is *old*? You've known each other long enough for him to call you his "alluring little airport pick-up", eh? At least, I think that was what he said, and I'll even go so far as to agree about the "alluring" bit. I was quite preoccupied with counting the number of vertebrae you have on exhibit, while you were busy on that goodnight embrace of yours,' he told her nastily.

'You – *oh*! You're despicable! I *knew* you would be, of course, even before I left London. You spied on me there, and you're doing it here, too, already! Why couldn't you have announced your presence when I came in, like any

44

decent man would, instead of lurking there like – like some – some second-rate private eye?'

He raised one eyebrow at this frontal attack. Rennie was amazed at the mobility and expressiveness of that bleached, jutting brow. It spoke volumes, and so did the angry glitter from the wide-set eyes that raked her greenly from head to toe, in a withering manner.

'Who's talking of decency? And what was I supposed to do? Blow a trumpet and break up the party?' he queried sarcastically. 'I was on my way to announce my presence, as you so delicately put it, when it was suddenly quite painfully evident that my presence was not exactly welcome. And when one finds oneself to be *persona non grata*, there's only one thing to do, and that is to lie doggo for a bit.'

'Doggo, indeed! You were eavesdropping!'

'Not intentionally. But I'll admit I heard everything that was said, so why bother pretending? The whole thing was cheap and sickening.'

Rennie gazed at him, in genuine distress now. There was no doubting his displeasure and disgust. The green eyes had narrowed into impenetrable slits that seemed to see both through and beyond her, his features had settled into their former mould of uncompromising sternness, and his mouth was positively forbidding.

Towering over her, with the darkness of the bedroom behind his wide, grey-clad shoulders, he appeared tough and accusing and not a little frightening.

She swallowed nervously. Suddenly, uncharacteristically, Rennie felt that she could quite easily have allowed herself the luxury of crying. That was what she was tempted to do – just cry, with tiredness and frustration and strangeness and despair – and if he were half a man, he might stop being quite so brutish, and comfort her instead. That was what almost any other man of Rennie's acquaintance would have done just then, and gladly, but instinct told her that *this* man was different. He didn't look the kind who'd suffer feminine weakness, either gladly or ungladly, and she certainly wasn't going to risk a rebuff.

45

Noting the defiant toss of her head, and the burning strain in her tense, paper-white face, he spoke gruffly.

'You'd better come through to the sitting-room. You look as if you could pass out, standing there, and a woman in a faint can be a damn nuisance.'

Rennie bit her lip vexedly, but she was glad, all the same, to follow him through the darkened bedroom to the small lounge beyond, where she sank thankfully against the cushions on the sofa.

The man hitched his trousers and took a chair near the reading lamp, where he had evidently been seated with a magazine when he had heard her key in the lock.

He flipped the magazine shut now, slapped it on the table.

'You'd better lie right back. Twelve thousand miles is a long way, with a night on the town right on top of it. It was madness, I reckon.' His deep voice was quiet now, just a little kinder.

Rennie blinked her stinging eyelids, and replied tremulously.

'I know that that's how it must look, and I can hardly expect you to believe me against the evidence of your own eyes and ears, but it's quite true, what I told you. Keith and I *are* old friends. Very – *dear* friends. I hadn't seen him for some time, though. We – we quarrelled, you see, over – well, it doesn't much matter what *over*, but we did. And when I bumped into him at Tahiti, and he asked me to come out, I – well–' she shrugged helplessly – 'you saw how it was.'

Even from this distance, she could feel that level green gaze dissecting her thoughtfully.

'It wasn't a pick-up, after all?'

'One is hardly in a position to pick up the *pilot*, Mr. Sandasen, when one is an aircraft passenger on an international flight,' she pointed out dryly.

'So that's what he is, an airline pilot! He had me puzzled, I'll admit.'

He stroked his tanned, clean-shaven chin consideringly. Rennie could see, by the small pool of light right beside him, that Chalford Sandasen had hands that were

46

broad-backed, strong and expressive, with long, flexible square-tipped fingers. Clever hands that matched the eagle alertness behind that lazy gaze and the athletic, deceptively loose-limbed build.

'He means a lot to you, then, this – er – pilot?' he asked at length, carefully.

Rennie hesitated.

What could she say? Deny it, and have him think that she had merely been philandering after all? Admit it, and expose herself to the taunts and teasing which she suspected must inevitably follow? There wasn't much choice, after all, was there? She was in an acutely vulnerable position, and it remained to be seen whether it was in him to be merciful.

'Yes,' she stated briefly, huskily, 'he does.'

There, it was done. Three people in the world now knew how much Keith Stamford meant to Rennie, and those three were Viv, Rennie herself, and this disturbing, domineering man whom she had known for barely a quarter of an hour! She hated him, now, for forcing the admission from her; hated him, for what he knew!

She glanced down at her hands, surprised to find that they were trembling. Rennie clasped her fingers tightly together so that he would not notice. She was unable to meet the man's eyes, although she was aware that he was studying her silently.

'That's a pity,' he remarked coolly – and wasn't there just the faintest hint of casual amusement there as well? – 'because I'm afraid that that impassioned goodnight in the lobby just now must be regarded as nothing less than a valediction – for the time being, anyway!'

'H-how do you mean?'

'I mean that, as things are, it was nothing short of a farewell, albeit a temporary one. A good thing I didn't interrupt it as I was tempted to do!'

'A *farewell*! But *why*?'

'We leave first thing in the morning,' stated Chalford Sandasen with characteristic directness. 'In precisely six hours from now,' he added, with a brief glance at the watch that was strapped to one hairy brown wrist.

'Leave? For where? Y-you mean, leave – *Sydney?*'

'But of course I mean leave Sydney. You don't suppose I intend to remain here a day longer than is necessary, do you? I mean to take Magda to her new home just as soon as possible – and you, too, perforce,' he reminded her sternly, as if sensing her mounting consternation.

Butterflies of sheer apprehension were fluttering around in Rennie's weary brain, muddling her thoughts. There was something here that she did not understand.

She sat up briskly, eyes opened wide.

'Where is home?' she managed to ask in what she hoped was an off-hand manner, just to show that she didn't *really* mind.

'Home?' The green eyes almost disappeared into those far-seeing, contemplative slits – *dreamy* slits. The stern angles of the man's face softened in the lamplight. 'Home is Barrindilloo, Miss Bentmore.'

She glanced at him suspiciously. He almost sounded as if he were playing with her, and quite enjoying it, too, although there was no doubting the affection with which he had spoken that strange-sounding name.

'Where is that?' she inquired cautiously.

'Oh, a good few hundred miles away from here. But in my plane it's no distance at all, of course. I've a rather nifty twin-engined Aztec sitting out there at the 'drome that's good at getting me places in a hurry. She'll take three easily, so you and Magda will be no problem.'

He got to his feet, yawned.

Rennie got to her feet too. Her voice was as tight as a fiddle-string.

'*Where?*' she asked again, and this time she could not even *pretend* not to care.

'Well, it's just this side of the Black Stump itself.'

He grinned down at her lazily. When he did that, deep crinkles appeared at the corners of those long, green eyes, and a sort of dimple indented his lean brown cheek. Just one cheek, it seemed to happen to. The left one, actually, because his smile was a lop-sided sort of one, and it was *that* side of his mouth that curled the most, too. It altered his whole face, somehow – that smile. Quite apart from

48

crinkling the level green eyes into laughing, teasing slits, it showed the whitest of teeth – a little bit crooked, but they all gleamed like pearl against his teak-brown, weathered cheeks – and when he raised one brow like that as well, the effect was mocking. *Maddeningly* mocking!

'The Black Stump?' Rennie's own eyes were demanding more information with unconcealed urgency. Actually, she was rooted to the spot where she stood, because she had a sudden strange, intuitive feeling that she was not going to like the information which she was about to receive.

She had to know, though.

He shrugged.

'Out where the crows fly backwards to keep the dust out of their eyes, and the goannas walk on their tails to stop their bellies from getting singed,' he elucidated calmly, holding her eyes with his.

'The—? You mean – the *country*?' she squeaked in horror.

What about those lovely beaches, where Magda was to get so brown and strong? What about the lovely sunshine and sand and sea air – and – everything?

Chalford Sandasen laughed – softly, so as not to awaken the sleeping child next door.

'If you take into account a mountain range or two, the odd river system, a spell of burnt, dry plain, a brief hop over gibber and saltbush and claypan country, a touch of spinifex, then up through the mulga for a bit – yes, I think you could call it "the country".' His lips twitched at her expression. 'The Outback is what *we* generally call it,' he informed her kindly, with commendable tolerance.

'The *Outback*! You aren't taking Magda out *there*? You – you're gammoning me!' she accused him fiercely.

The bleached eyebrow shot up.

'You learn *fast*, Miss Bentmore! But no, I am not gammoning you. That is indeed where I am taking Magda. And you, too. For three months, isn't it?' he reminded her carelessly.

'Over my dead body,' announced Rennie firmly.

49

'We've been misled. You've *deceived* us!' She glared at him. 'I really wonder that your wife permitted it. You'd think that she, at least, would have realized what it might mean to pack up our things and come all the way across the world like this on a w-wild goose chase!'

Calm green eyes locked with angry brown.

'There's no question of a wild goose chase, Miss Bentmore. And what's more, I don't have a wife.'

'No – no *wife*!' To Rennie this was the ultimate, the final, crime. 'No wife? But – but who'll look after Magda? Who'll bring her up? Who'll comfort her, and keep her, and bandage her up when she skins her knees – she's always having accidents – she's accident-*prone*, you see – and she gets nosebleeds, too. And who'll hear her prayers, and kiss her goodnight, and help her with her homework, and – oh, a thousand things a little girl needs and wants? Who'll do them, out in those w-waterless wastes, with not even a w-*wife*? Who'll *do* them, out where the crows fly backwards and the goannas – *goannas*—!' Rennie's voice rose to a shriek.

'What devotion! Especially from you, Miss Bentmore. *You*, who were more than willing to abandon her in a strange city on her very first night. *You*, who put her into children's homes without a single qualm, while you go gallivanting off to the sun yourself on that frivolous career of yours.'

'Who'll *do* them?'

'Hush!' said the man sternly. '*I* will.'

'*You* will?'

'*I* will.'

Rennie took a deep breath, and squared her shoulders.

'I'm not going to allow Magda to go out there, Mr. Sandasen,' she told him stoutly. 'I am going to keep Magda with me, and we'll go on as we have before. I'll get work, and I can support us like I always have. Eventually I'll get us back to England, back where we came from, to civilization. It might not be too easy, and I know it's not ideal, my way of life, but at least it's better than abandoning her to – to *that*!'

Chalford Sandasen shook his head. His expression was such that it struck chill to Rennie's very heart. His tough, lean face had congealed into an uncompromising granite mask, his mouth had levelled to a thin, straight line, and his eyes had paled to a cool, unfriendly grey.

'You, Miss Bentmore,' he corrected her relentlessly, 'will do no such thing. Kindly remember that you are in Australia now, a visitor – without citizenship, without rights. You have little means of support, and can claim only a distant relationship with the child, who is my own late brother's daughter, and therefore legally my own niece. I can knock any claim you make into a cocked hat, and you know it – dismantle any argument you choose to employ, and you know that, too. What's more, I shan't hesitate to do it, at court-appeal level, if necessary. Therefore Magda *will* come with me to Barrindilloo tomorrow, and so will you. And Magda will *remain*.'

Rennie's colour was high, her breath coming fast. How she'd have liked the satisfaction of hitting him, of slapping that hard, tanned, supercilious cheek!

She raised a hand, dropped it impotently, uselessly. And then, in sheer outrage and frustration, she did the very thing which she had determined *not* to do, the thing she had been trying *not* to do – something, indeed, that she had seldom done in her whole life. She burst into tears.

Stricken with shame, she put her hands over her face and bowed her head, so that the man would not see. She wept then, quietly, with tiny, almost noiseless sobs.

To her horror, she found that, now she had begun, she could not stop. Rennie wasn't quite sure exactly what she was crying for. An accumulation of things, maybe. For the loss of her father's quiet affection and his last unhappy years with Enid. For Magda with her poor little scarred, scared face, and her poor little battered one-eyed panda. For herself. For Keith. For the very hopelessness of the whole situation. Because she knew now that she had made a dreadful mistake in coming out here at all, that she wasn't going to let Magda go. She *couldn't*, could she? Not to a life like *that*? And that, in its turn, meant

51

that Keith – that Keith – just when she had met him again – had thought herself *free*—

Hot tears forced their way through her fingers and ran in channels down her cheeks, and then Rennie felt herself being drawn against a broad, grey-suited chest. One of the man's hands moved quite expertly over her slim brown shoulder-blades and down her back, and the other drew her head firmly against the place where Chalford Sandasen's clean white shirt-front met the neat low-cut lapels of his elegant, single-breasted pale grey jacket.

While she fought to control this awful, abandoned fit of sobbing, she could hear his deep voice murmuring above her head, while his supple fingers stroked the gentle curve at her nape with a soothing touch that was at once kind and impersonal.

'You're overwrought, child. You should have been in bed hours ago, like little Magda there. You know, you mustn't worry about what I've told you. You don't need to worry, you can leave everything to me now, and I'll take care of her, I promise you. I was only teasing about the country, but I can see you're really quite scared about it, aren't you? Those lawyers were supposed to tell you, but maybe they didn't, or maybe you didn't read it properly. Anyway, there's no need to be concerned about Barrindilloo. It's far out, yes, but it weaves its spell. The Outback always does, you know. It enmeshes people in its magic and wonder and vastness, so that they never want to leave it, and the ones who do leave it almost always want to come back.

> 'And I crossed again
> Over the miles of saltbush plain,
> The shining plain that is said to be
> The dried-up bed of an inland sea.'

They always come back, you know. They all cross again, and again. It's because of the fascination, and the magical quality of the great Australian bush. It's something you can't explain, but you become a part of it. It's a good place for a kid to grow up in, too. Magda will grow into a beaut little Australian, you bet she will – and in just three months you'll be able to leave her – sooner, if she settles down quickly – and by the look of things that pilot chap'll be waiting to—'

Rennie stiffened at that, and tried to push herself away, recalling just where she was, and precisely whose chest she was leaning against in this limp, abandoned fashion – the man who had cheated her, who had misled her so cruelly, who was even now planning to incarcerate little Magda in some godforsaken, treeless prison out at the back of nowhere.

Chalford Sandasen stepped back, but, as if sensing her thoughts, he took care to retain his grasp upon both her wrists. He jerked them suddenly, angrily, forcing her to look up into his face.

'Don't fight me, Renata Bentmore,' he warned her sternly, and his eyes were gimlet hard, like chips of ice, his touch no longer gentle. 'If you do, you'll only hurt yourself, because I always fight to win. Understand?'

Something in his tone forced Rennie to nod her head with patent unwillingness. It was a weary gesture, but defiance still lingered.

He studied her ravaged face for a moment more, and then he released her, brought a flat, silver-mounted flask from a hip pocket, and poured a measure of the contents into the cup.

'You'd better drink that.'

'I never touch spirits.'

'There's a time and a place for everything – even spirits,' he replied expressionlessly. Then – *'Drink* it!'

Rennie shot him a quick, scared glance, and swallowed it at a single gulp.

He waited, unmoved, while she coughed and spluttered, then, noting her returning colour with satisfaction, he slipped the flask away again and said equably, 'That's better. I want you out there all in one piece at the 'drome in the morning. And try not to let the child sense that you're in any way upset or apprehensive, will you? Kids catch on to these things quickly. Goodnight.'

He was gone before Rennie could even muster a reply.

She undressed, slipped into her pyjamas and removed her make-up with automatic thoroughness, brushed her long fair hair until it shone with that incredible, gilded pallor that made professional photographers gasp and look again.

Rennie climbed carefully into the unoccupied bed beside Magda's twin one and lay back, thinking. She was glad, now, that the man had forced her to swallow his revolting brandy. It had pulled her together. Even now, she could feel its warmth reviving her, coursing through her veins, helping her to think calmly.

She knew what she intended to do. It shouldn't be too difficult, either. All she had to do was to make certain that she did not oversleep, or her whole plan would be ruined. It might be better if she didn't go to sleep at all, in fact, because the success of her entire plan depended upon getting out of here before Chalford Sandasen came back.

After that, they would simply disappear, she and Magda. Contrary to what he believed, Rennie had enough money with her to see them both over the time it would take to find employment. If it turned out that work permits were necessary, she'd abandon the idea of a professional job with its attendant possibility of publicity and detection, and settle for anything at all. She was strong, and she could clean or scrub or something, or maybe even try some simple cooking. So long as she could keep the little girl with her, Rennie didn't much mind *what* she did! Magda would be able to remain in Sydney, and she would be able to go to school, just as all the other thousands of little Australians no doubt did. In Rennie's free time, they would make straight for those lovely beaches, play on that fine white sand, swim in that sparkling blue Pacific. And eventually they would get back to England. Viv would be willing to help in that way, she was almost sure.

With her, Magda would remain secure and happy, Rennie would see to that. She need never know how near she had been to a life of desolation and loneliness, shut away in isolation with a harsh, domineering bachelor uncle who talked of crows flying backwards and goannas that walked on their tails. Ugh!

And he had said that that sort of thing *grew* on one, so that one never wanted to leave it. Some story, that! What he probably really meant was that, once he got you out there, he would not allow you to leave it! He had every intention of keeping Magda a prisoner there, all her life!

Well, Rennie's confessed intention was to thwart *his* intention.

She was pleased with herself for having thought up this plan with the aid of his own stimulating dose of spirits. A nice touch of irony, that was!

She slipped out of bed again, checked her watch, and went through to the small sitting-room. There she switched on the lamp, and began determinedly to read. She had worked out that she must have roughly three hours to fill in before daylight, and she did not dare allow herself to go to sleep. She was by now so tired that she realized, if she did drop off to sleep, that it might be a very long time indeed before she woke up again! Too long, probably!

She leafed her way blearily through a pile of well-thumbed magazines and periodicals. Nervousness, temerity at her own audacious plan, determination kept her from dozing off.

When the first grey hint of light appeared at the window, and the first sounds of the day-staff coming on duty reached her ears, Rennie shut the magazine which she had been reading with growing disinterest, and replaced it and the rest of the pile on the small coffee table. Then she went through to the bedroom and packed her evening dress and the other things which she had worn for her outing with Keith. She did not dare to allow herself even to think of him. Thinking hurt. Circumstances were now exactly as they had been before, as far as he and she were concerned, after all, weren't they? It was 'Rennie and Magda' – not 'Rennie alone' – and she wasn't going to risk all that heartache over again. But it was difficult, all the same, simply to close one's mind to all those freshly-awakened emotions and implications.

Rennie dressed with speed, and then woke Magda. The child was refreshed after her sleep, bubbling over with high spirits and excitement.

'Oh, Rennie, isn't it big! Is it *all* Sydney out there?'

'All Sydney, darling, yes. Quickly, Magda, let's get your clothes on. We're going exploring this morning.'

'Exploring? Out there?' Magda waved a small hand sideways at the vista beyond the window. 'How super, Rennie! Can we see a beach? Can we walk on one? *Play* on one?'

'We *might*,' replied Rennie cautiously. 'Hurry, though.'

'Can we eat first? I'm hungry.'

Rennie smiled. It was good to hear that Magda was hungry. Her appetite had been poor for a long time now, and she was so pale and thin that it worried Rennie constantly. Perhaps the change of scene and air were helping already. Perhaps the journey would not have been for nothing, after all!

Even so, she shook her head.

'We'll have breakfast later, darling. Somewhere different. Somewhere exciting.'

'Where?'

'Somewhere *secret*, not in this building at all. I mean, we ate here yesterday, anyway, didn't we? We're going somewhere different.'

Magda scented mystery. Her eyes began to sparkle.

'Ooh, great!' she voted enthusiastically, and made more haste with her dressing than before.

Her eyes widened when she saw Rennie heaving the three suitcases in the direction of the lift.

'We aren't taking those, are we? Not *exploring*?'

'We're going to leave them somewhere, and *then* go exploring.'

'Why not here?'

'No, not here,' said Rennie quickly. *Anywhere* but here, she thought a little desperately. Somewhere where she could claim them later without arousing curiosity or risking detection. A railway station, maybe. That would be an anonymous sort of place. But first she had to get them downstairs.

'You wait here with the hand-luggage, Magda. I'll order a taxi at the reception desk, and then I'll come back for you. Sit there and play with Panda for a minute. Tell him what we're going to do, and think about what you want for breakfast when the time comes. I'll get you a really big breakfast today, if you're hungry – at the secret place!'

A minute or two later Rennie lifted the cases over to the reception desk, and asked if it would be possible to obtain a taxi at such an early hour. She almost sighed audibly with sheer relief at the affirmative reply she received.

'Certainly, madam. Just ask the hall porter over there, will you?'

'A taxi? Yes, of course, miss. Is that your luggage there? Just the three pieces, is it? I'll take care of it.'

'And I've a few things yet upstairs. I shan't be a moment.'

Rennie turned in a hurry, cannoned precipitately into the tall, khaki-clad figure standing right behind her.

Chalford Sandasen steadied her by the simple expedient of gripping both her arms in a vice-like hold. His fingers bit cruelly into her soft flesh as he restored her balance, and looked down.

'Going somewhere? I don't *think* so!' The green eyes were curiously hard as he answered his own question.

'Cancel Madam's taxi, will you, Enrico? The lady has changed her mind,' he told the porter calmly.

'And the cases, Mr. Sandasen?'

'No, you can leave them where they are. We'll be checking out shortly.'

'Very good, sir. Thank *you*, Mr. Sandasen!'

Enrico pocketed his tip and retired discreetly behind a potted palm in the forecourt, and Rennie was left standing in that sea of marble foyer, alone with Chalford Sandasen.

Right now she was receiving such a keen and estimating assessment that it made her prickle with guilt

57

and embarrassment.

'You weren't thinking of running out on me, by any chance, Renata?' he drawled in amusement. The unexpected and deliberate use of her christian name seemed to bring her even closer to her persecutor. 'It must have taken you the rest of the night to hatch up this one! I can see you haven't slept a wink!'

'Oh, go *away*!' Rennie stamped her foot in sheer vexation.

'Now, that's just the one thing I won't do, I'm afraid,' he told her regretfully, but his eyes mocked, and there was a nasty lift to the mobile mouth too. 'And neither will you – or not just yet, at any rate. When we go, Renata, we'll go together, do you understand? You, me, and Magda. I must congratulate you on your effort, though,' he added graciously. 'It was a pretty fair try, in fact. A pity your dawn-time vigil was all for nothing, but I have an inconvenient habit of waking round about piccaninny daylight, and it did pass through my mind that you might attempt something of this sort.'

'I think you're smug and insufferable!' Rennie informed him with a look of pure loathing.

'And *I* think *you* are too tired and confused to give a worthwhile opinion,' he replied evenly. 'Now, go and get Magda, will you, please, and join me for breakfast in the dining-room. I was half-way through when you went sneaking past. I reckon my steak and eggs will be cold by now. Come straight to the table, and don't try to bolt again, will you? I might not be quite so forbearing the next time!'

Rennie turned on her heel, speechless, still seething.

'Oh – and Renata?'

'Yes?'

Grinning, he pointed to the three large suitcases.

'Next time you try to do a Malley's Cow, my advice is to go light-on with the trappings. You hadn't a hope in Hades with that lot, plus a kid!'

She walked in huffy silence to the lift, ignored the soft chuckle that followed her before he went back into the dining-room. When she returned with Magda, he got to his feet, seated Rennie herself and then the child.

'This is Mr. Sandasen, Magda.'

'Hullo there.' He looked down at the pale, upturned face with its angry red scars, still liverishly evident. 'So you're Magda, eh? How old are you, Magda? Six?'

'Seven.'

'Seven.' He resumed his seat. 'At the very peak of female wisdom, I should say. After that, their judgment begins to deteriorate' – this with a meaning glance in Rennie's direction. 'Are you hungry, Magda?'

'Yes, Mr. Sandasen.'

'You'd better call me Chad,' he told her carelessly, and smiled in a sudden fascinating, eye-crinkling way that Magda appeared to like. 'Have you got it? Chad? Everyone calls me that, from here right up to the Gulf. So you'd better do it, too.'

'Yes, Chad.'

'And you are hungry, you say? That's good! What would you like?'

'I could eat a horse,' announced Magda with unaccustomed enthusiasm.

'A horse? Well, they mightn't have an actual *horse* listed here, Magda, but there's plenty of number one tucker, all the same.'

Chad leaned over, a brown finger following the words with Magda, as he read out the menu.

When he had ascertained her choice, he turned to Rennie.

'And for you?'

'I'm not hungry,' Rennie stated dully, and it was certainly no more than the truth.

He took in the whiteness about her wilful, expertly rouged mouth, the smudges under the sherry-brown eyes that even Rennie's skilled professional hand could not entirely conceal.

'You're going to eat something, all the same.'

He ordered for them both, poured himself another cup of coffee, caught Magda's eye and grinned conspiratorially, and the child smiled back.

'I like it here, with you,' she averred solemnly.

Oh, Magda! Rennie cast her a reproachful glance, which was entirely lost upon its recipient. Magda beamed, and continued with bland and fetching innocence.

'I didn't think I'd be here for breakfast, Chad. Me an' Rennie was going somewhere else to have it, weren't we, Rennie? Somewhere *secret*.'

'Were you, indeed?' came that deep interested murmur – smooth as cream, and Rennie knew, without even having to look, that one eyebrow would have lifted quizzically as he said the word. She kept her eyes down, scarlet-faced.

'Why didn't we go, after all, Rennie? To the secret place?' inquired Magda curiously.

'I – we – because I met your uncle Chad – a bit unexpectedly, Magda, and I decided we'd have breakfast here instead. It was one of those sudden decisions. We weren't to know that we would run into Chad when we decided to go to the secret place, were we?' she replied as calmly as she could.

'No, we *weren't*, were we?' muttered the man at her side, so softly that only she could catch the words. 'And we're still very angry that we *did* run into him, aren't we, Renata? But we mustn't sulk over breakfast, all the same. Another piece of toast?' he queried, in normal tones.

'No, thank you,' she snapped repressively, hating him more with every minute that passed.

Already he had managed to win over Magda, with a snap of the fingers, just like that! One crinkle-green glance, a crumpled smile, a little charming patter and – pouf! – a small, silent worshipper had been enslaved. Why, right at this minute they were busy smiling away at each other with mutual abandonment, oblivious to the fact that there was a third person at this table at all!

'I'm ready,' said Rennie, in a small, pale voice.

'Right. In that case, we'll go.' He turned to Magda. 'I'm going to take you home now, Magda. Home to Barrindilloo. You'll like it there. There's lots of sunshine, and places to swim, and I'll show you how to catch fish in the pool in the creek. There are horses to ride, and sometimes poddies to feed. Real kangaroos and emus. And in the evening the little ringtail possums come out to feed on the gum-leaves, and the bush is filled with all the strange little noises of the night-feeding animals and birds. We'll sit out under the stars, you and I, and I'll tell you what every one of those sounds is, so that you'll know them, too, and each creature that makes them. And there are lots of people at Barrindilloo, too, friends just waiting for you to come. They know all about you, although you don't yet know *them*. They know your name and everything, and they're looking forward to the moment when you step down on to the strip, because they know you've come a long, long way already, right across the world from London, and that when you step down on to that airstrip, you'll be home. Now there's just a little way further to travel. We're going to do it in my plane, which is out at the 'drome waiting for us. You won't mind a ride in another plane, will you, Magda? A smaller one, this time?'

'Not if Rennie comes too,' said Magda immediately, and just then her small fingers closed convulsively over Rennie's own hand in a heart-warming way that, to Rennie, was a reward in itself. 'You are coming, aren't you, Rennie?'

'Yes, darling, of *course* I'm coming,' replied Rennie reassuringly. Somehow she even managed a stiff, awkward smile, and over the top of Magda's small head her eyes sought Chad Sandasen's. They were already fixed upon her with a look that was green and inscrutable.

'Cheer up,' he murmured sleekly, as Magda ran ahead. 'Three months soon passes!'

In some inexplicable way, that remark had a curiously challenging and bracing effect, just when her resolution was threatening to wobble. As she walked by his side to the waiting taxi, Rennie felt her spine stiffening, her chin tilting, in response.

CHAPTER FOUR

RENNIE had to move nearer to Magda to allow Chad Sandasen into the taxi beside her, since both the boot and the front seat beside the driver were taken up with luggage – their own, and a masculine-looking rawhide case which Enrico had brought out and placed beside the rest.

Her eyes slid sideways, took in the pale drill trousers, the many-pocketed khaki shirt of the man who was of necessity sitting much too near to her for Rennie's liking.

The shirt was informal, short-sleeved, and she was acutely aware of the muscular strength of those impossibly brown, bare forearms as Chad Sandasen rested his hands forward on his knees in the confined space. Beside his, Rennie's own slender limbs, of whose tan she had been justly proud back there in England, appeared ridiculously pale by comparison.

At the throat of his shirt was a cravat of fine cotton, brightly printed, carelessly tied.

'At the risk of interrupting your inspection, Renata, may I point out the Harbour Bridge over there? And that odd-shaped building on the water-line is our new Opera House – both landmarks worthy of a tourist's attention, I should say.'

'I – oh, yes, I see them. Thank you.' She had been caught, and the knowledge made her suddenly shy. 'I can believe that you're a countryman today, in – I – I mean – in those clothes,' she muttered uncomfortably, reddening as she saw the way that eyebrow shot up, and the tiny lights of amusement began to leap in his narrowing green look.

He shrugged.

'You had me labelled as a city slicker, had you? I'm sorry to have disappointed you, Renata.' A grin. 'You're obviously at home with the type.'

She bit her lip, flushing angrily. If that was meant as a dig at Keith, she was going to do the dignified thing, and ignore it.

'I can be forgiven for assuming that you were a city man, I think,' she defended herself, 'since the only communications I had from you were all from Sydney. And even when we arrived yesterday, Mr. Krantz told us that you were "out of town". That, surely, implied that you were normally to be found *in* town?'

'I spend a certain amount of time in cities, one way and another, so Krantz's implication was not entirely unfounded. I regret the misunderstanding, however. I was actually down at the Cup for a few days.'

'The Cup? What's that?'

'The Melbourne Cup. You must have heard of it, surely?'

'A – a competition of some sort?' she hazarded.

'Good God, girl! A *race*!'

'A *horse* race?' Rennie glared at him with open disapproval. 'Gambling? A lonely property at the back of beyond, no wife, no experience of children, and now a – a self-confessed gambler! And you have the nerve to think that you're better qualified than I to—'

'Sh!' He frowned meaningfully in Magda's direction, but his eyes were mocking her at the same time. 'My dear Renata, the Melbourne Cup is one of the most famous races in the whole *world*. A two-mile handicap that has produced some legendary accomplishments in staying power. Haven't you ever heard of the mighty Phar Lap? The magnificent Carbine? The indomitable Peter Pan? Rain Lover? Delta? Or that gallant, wonderful little mare, Light Fingers, who *won* the crowd even when she *lost* the race?' He shook his head reproachfully. 'It's not a form of gambling. It's an institution. It's patriotism, nothing less!'

'Patriotism! You can't dismiss it as easily as that,' Rennie told him scornfully, quelling her conscience as she recalled the number of times that she herself had attended fashionable Ascot in the company of one or another of her numerous male admirers.

A rather nasty gleam in his eye made her wonder if he could possibly have read her mind.

'Your puritanical reactions interest me, Renata,' he murmured silkily. 'I'm tempted to confess to various of my other vices, just for the hell of watching your response, do you know that!' And then, offhandedly – 'What else did Krantz have to tell you?'

'Oh, nothing, really,' she replied airily.

Just that everyone calls you 'Chad', she could have told him, but refrained. Just that you're the Boss, in spite of them calling you that. At the top of the pyramid. Like a Pharaoh with his slaves, whatever Mr. Krantz might have said about 'respect' and 'affection'.

'You'll see what I mean in time,' Mr. Krantz had said. 'You'll be calling him Chad yourself.'

And she *was* calling him Chad, already, just like all those people from here to the Gulf, wherever that was. She could concede that particular point to Mr. Krantz willingly enough, but *never* the other, *never* that bit about respect and affection. You didn't feel respect and affection for a man who had dragged you half around the world in that high-handed manner, who had deceived you, spied on you, teased you, thwarted you, and finally *forced* you to eat the breakfast you didn't want so that you'd be fit enough to travel in his beastly little aeroplane to his horrid big property in the horrid, even *bigger* Outback.

The beastly little aeroplane turned out to be a silver-winged and graceful beauty.

Chad Sandasen pulled off his cravat, threw it on to a rack, unbuttoned his shirt to the waist, and stowed the gear. Then he saw his passengers strapped into their seats comfortably, and made the routine pre-flight checks with quiet efficiency.

And then they were airborne, ascending into the wide blue, cloudless skies of the Southern Cross, and Rennie could only suppose that they must seem to the ground-dweller like a mere distant silver speck in the bright azure dome overhead.

Certainly, from above, eternity itself appeared to be

64

spread out below – the never-ending vastness of the great Australian hinterland in all its varying wonder. Towering, jungly ranges with plunging purple gullies and crumbling russet gorges; patchwork quilts of crop and orchard; quiet rivers and willow-fringed creeks; barren stretches of plain, the dotted saltbush, the steely bluebush, the lonely gibber; thirsty channels that fossicked amongst parched mosaics of cracked mud; the claypan deserts; then the saltbush again, and stunted stands of mulga; in and out over belah and brigalow. For a time, the railway, with tiny sidings, infrequently spaced, and the isolated fettler's hut; wells and windmills; bores and ground-tanks and turkey-nest dams; the mulga again.

And then – Barrindilloo.

Rennie could see the name quite clearly beneath them, painted in large black lettering on a long galvanized roof. They descended to the adjacent airstrip, bumped gently over the hard-baked ground, finally stopped, and as she and Magda were helped down from the plane, the heat waves seemed to rise up from the earth and beat at her face, with noiseless, relentless buffetings.

Rennie gasped. She felt hot and tired and wilted, and the defiance had momentarily gone out of her. She realized that her wool jersey outfit had been a mistake. It clung and prickled, and tiny rivulets of perspiration ran down her skin underneath it. Chad, on the other hand, appeared not to even notice the temperature. She looked away from his tanned, hair-covered barrel of chest, exposed by the opened safari-shirt, to the man who had walked out of the nearby hangar and over to the strip to meet them.

Another khaki figure, in sagging trousers and the same elastic-sided stockman's boots as Chad Sandasen's own. He was elderly, with a heavily weathered countenance and shrewd, dark eyes. A dependable sort of man. The level-headed type.

But – just one man, thought Rennie. No other people at all. Where, then, were all the friends whom Chad had promised for Magda? Was it just another of his calculated and shameless deceptions?

' 'Day, Chad. 'Ow was it, then? Someone give yer the good oil, did they?'

'The Cup?' Chad's lean face broke into a grin. He had reached into the cockpit for his wide-brimmed hat, which he now clapped down over his eyes at such an angle that all Rennie could see was the tip of his nose and that readily curving mouth. 'Not bad, Murtie. How did it go here?'

'Bennie won the sweep, the lucky cow. I drew Black Bandetto m'self. Of all the crook breaks a bloke can get! I never did trust a black horse, any'ow, and 'e finished last, like I might've guessed. G'day, ma'am' – This last remark was addressed to Rennie herself. It was accompanied by a courteous touch of gnarled fingers to the brim of his own wide-brimmed felt – a slightly battered replica of Chad's – and a solemn wink in Magda's direction.

'Miss Bentmore, Murtie. I'm sure she won't object to you calling her Renata. Murtie is my head stockman,' he went on to explain to the newcomers, 'and we all use first names out here.'

'And this here's Magda, Chad? Reckon she's got her pa's eyes, ain't she! The same blue as what Neil's were, eh?'

'Maybe, Murt.' The curling mouth tightened suddenly. Chad Sandasen bent down, picked up the little girl, lifted her into his arms in a single easy, sweeping movement. 'Let's have a look at you, Magda.'

The child submitted to a critical inspection as those strangely penetrating green eyes roved her face.

'Blue as periwinkles, aren't they, scrap?' His fingers chucked her chin playfully, and then ran gently, consideringly, along the angry, puckered lines of those thin, fine scars. 'And these will soon go, Magda. The sun and the clean, dry air will see to that! Very soon the marks will heal and fade, and you'll be the prettiest little poppet in the whole wide world, do you know that?'

He had spoken quite naturally, had chosen actually to draw attention to Magda's disfigurement, rather than pretend that it did not exist. Rennie felt indignation welling up inside her at his tactlessness. He was a brutal man, she knew, but surely he could have curbed his sadistic tendencies in the child's presence?

Now she held her breath, a tightness inside her as she suffered on Magda's behalf.

To her surprise, Magda beamed.

'Will I *really* be pretty, Chad?' she asked, doubtfully, wistfully, *hopefully*.

'Of course. Haven't I just said so?' His white, crooked teeth showed fleetingly in his swarthily tanned face. Rennie still could not see his eyes, only the square line of his jaw and the brown base of his throat as he brought the little girl's fingers up to the side of his lean, clean-shaven chin. 'See, I have one too. Right down there, but you've got to look hard to spot it, because the sun healed it all up, just as it will yours.'

And then she saw, as Magda was seeing, the thin, jagged seam that ran from Chad Sandasen's ear, right down the side of his cheek. It must have been an ugly wound at the time, for even now the line had a ragged edge to it at the jaw-line and then continued for a couple of inches down the side of the neck. For all that, it was barely discernible unless one looked closely as Magda was doing right now.

Her small fingers followed it to its conclusion near Chad's khaki shirt-collar.

'How did you do it?' she asked wonderingly. 'Will mine truly look like that one day?'

He laughed, shrugged carelessly as he set her on her feet again.

'A micky bull did it, Magda, a long time ago. I went into the scrub after him, and my horse came down. If I'd got clear in time, I might have thrown him as he charged, but he beat me to it, so to speak. Your own scars will be much, much less noticeable than that one, because you had a clever doctor to fix yours, and I only had Murtie here.'

'Aw, fair go, Boss!' protested that individual hotly. 'I did a decent job, I reckon, considerin' the equipment on hand at the time. If you remember, I was all for callin' up the Flyin' Doctor – but 'e wouldn't hear of it, see.' Murtie appealed to Rennie for support. 'Not in the middle of a bangtail muster, 'e wouldn't hear of it. Expected me ter do the honours, back at camp – and when Chad says *do* a thing, well,' – a lift of thickset shoulders – 'I reckon it's best just to get on an' *do* it.'

'Good advice, Renata,' murmured Chad Sandasen into her ear, as he took her arm, and turned her towards the house. There was an ironic gleam in the eyes that glanced down at her, taking in the weary pallor, the beads of perspiration on her brow. 'Right now you look as submissive as it's been my pleasure to see you! You'd better get out of this sun, and into something cooler. I presume you bought hats for yourself and Magda?'

'Of course,' she returned coldly. '*Beach* hats, to wear on those lovely Sydney beaches, remember?'

'Touché,' he grinned. 'Well, you'll just have to come to terms with yourself about that, I'm afraid. You can take your choice of the creek or the tank for swimming, but we don't have beaches on Barrindilloo, do we, Murtie?'

'Reckon we don't, Chad,' Murtie agreed hesitantly. It was obvious that the admission was wrung from him reluctantly, that Barrindilloo was very close to his heart indeed, and that he did not like to think it could possibly be lacking in anything at all. 'What's the use o' them fancy beaches anyway, with sheilas lollin' around sunnin' themselves and makin' free with all those fancy creams an' stuff? Here, you don't need to go sun-worshippin', Renata, and lookin' out fer the sun like they do on those beaches. *Here* the sun looks out fer *you*, and it'll find what it's lookin' for quick enough without *you* even *tryin'*! You take care, or that lovely peaches-'n-cream of yours'll end up as burnt and brown as a scrubber's hide, ain't that so, Chad?'

'Very probably, Murt, except that Renata might not be here for very long.'

'Well, you go ahead an' I'll bring that gear up in the jeep. S'long, Magda. S'long for now, Renata.'

'Er – so long, Murtie.'

Rennie smiled, because she had taken an immediate and unexpected liking to this quaint old man.

The stockman's eyes lit up appreciatively. 'Some name,

that *Renata*,' he murmured admiringly. 'It's got class, I reckon. Kind of *thoroughbred*, like one of those fillies you were watchin' runnin' in the Cup, eh, Boss?' He sighed. 'All them thoroughbreds, and *I* had ter draw a mongrel like Black Bandetto! I never took to a black horse yet, nor one of them ter me. Come ter think of it, it was a black brute went down on you in the scrub that time, Chad. That vicious colt off Satan's Whiskers, you recall?'

'I recall.' The other's brevity was not intended to be encouraging, but Murtie didn't appear to notice.

'Give me a thoroughbred filly any day, Chad, eh! I always did like a palomino too – and so did you!' he asserted enthusiastically, with a meaning glance at Rennie's shining curtain of pale, beautiful hair. 'Just anything you want, Renata – you or Magda – you just ask old Murtie and it's yours, see. If you find yourself wonderin' about anythin', you just come to Murtie. I know every inch of this station, an' I'll be pleased ter show you round.'

'It seems you've got yourself an admirer,' remarked Chad Sandasen coolly as they walked the short distance to the homestead.

'I don't need admirers, thank you,' Rennie retorted crisply. 'I'm more in need of *allies*.'

'Then don't think that you will find them amongst my staff,' he warned her abruptly. 'They're completely loyal. Come, Magda.' He turned to the little girl, lifted her into his arms, and smiled, a smile of warmth and spontaneity, a smile of affection and genuine welcome, of pleasure and of justifiable pride. 'This is your new home, Magda, and I know that you and I are going to be very happy here together.'

You and I.

Rennie, alone, walked behind them through a small gate in a dazzlingly white picket fence, and over the sweeping green lawns that surrounded the homestead at Barrindilloo, trying not to notice the way in which that tall, spare figure in front was giving all his attention to the excited child whom he had now perched atop his soulder. His strides were long and casual and loping, and they took himself and Magda away from Rennie so that she could no longer catch what they were saying to each other, but she could see Chad's long arm pointing to something as he stood for a moment for Magda to look, and then she heard Magda's childish laughter ringing out.

Rennie tried not to notice. She tried not to notice the beauty that surrounded her, either. What if the lawns were so verdant and close-cropped and extensive? It didn't change anything, not one jot. This place at the back of beyond was not suitable for Magda at all!

Rennie tried to ignore the spilling shrubberies of oleander and acacia and grevillea, of hibbertia and bougainvillea, the colourful beds of portulaca and canna, of iris and leschenaultia, the cool, whispering screen of taller eucalypts and pines beyond, which threw a dappled shade over the path up which she walked.

At the veranda steps a mound of pig-face made a splash of vibrant purple against the neighbouring clumps of silver-foliaged white daisies, and a trellis of vines screened a wide, dark porch.

At the top of the steps, Chad Sandasen lifted Magda from his shoulders, took off his wide-brimmed hat, and held open the gauze-meshed door, indicating that they should enter. Rennie could feel his eyes upon her face, but she could not meet them. With a wooden expression, she stepped through the doorway and into the house.

So it was beautiful, but it still didn't change anything.

Cool and sumptuous, traditional in style, modern in comfort.

Cane loungers and deck-chairs, small wicker tables and a bookcase gave the enclosed veranda the appearance of an outer, casual living-room.

Inside, there were high ceilings, waxed pine floors, richly textured rugs, and substantial, cool leather chairs. A room with a tall, colonial marble fireplace, a vast rectangular table, high-backed chairs – the dining-room. Another with pretty elegant furniture, antique mirrors, tapestry cushions on a soft, somewhat shabby, sofa, and

70

another of those generous mantelpieces over which, this time, was set an oil portrait. Rennie glimpsed it in passing – a woman's face, with the same high, intelligent forehead as Chad Sandasen's own. The hair was the same, too – crisp and brown and abundant, although without those lighter, sun-bleached streaks of his. The eyes were not long and green and speculative. They were piercingly blue and bright and inquisitive. Neil's eyes, perhaps? Or Magda's.

Rennie swallowed.

The legitimacy, the extent, of this man's claim upon Magda was evident in that portrait – patently, incontrovertibly evident.

Had that vivacious blue-eyed woman been younger, she could have been Magda's own mother, for the child did not resemble Betty in looks at all. And when Magda herself grew into middle age, it was not inconceivable that she might resemble that portrait to an extraordinary degree. Magda, in looks, was all Sandasen, and Rennie had a feeling that that fact alone was going to make her own arguments over the child's guardianship less convincing, more difficult.

Even so, what could this man offer? A lonely existence in the isolation of the Outback, on a vast cattle run where the only person whom Rennie had so far seen, other than Chad, was an ageing stockman who confessed to a distaste of black horses and a liking for palominos, and the only apparent means of entry and exit appeared to be a sleek silver aeroplane that swooped down out of the sky into a veritable township of iron-roofed buildings and sheds – uninhabited, unmanned.

Worse still, un*woman*ed!

She cleared her throat, which was dusty and dry.

'Where is everyone?' she asked doubtfully. 'Where are all the people of whom you spoke? The – the *friends*?'

'Magda's friends?' His voice was cool, his eyes hard. 'If you think I invented them, Renata, I'm afraid you're doomed to disappointment. I've no intention of providing you with ammunition to shoot down my own case!' He

71

glanced after Magda's distant figure, excitedly exploring, before adding bluntly, 'You don't trust me an inch, do you?'

'Should I?'

Her chin tilted stubbornly.

'It's not important, but it could have been helpful, all the same.' He was looking at her in a strange but unfathomable way. It made Rennie feel suddenly, acutely uncomfortable. 'On the question of Magda, Renata, neither your trust nor your liking is essential, and there can only be one outcome, one conclusion, so far as she is concerned.'

'We can decide that in three months' time.'

'On the contrary, it's already decided. And you're under no obligation to remain here for the full three months, if Magda settles down quickly. I dare say you're even now breaking your neck to get back to Sydney to that *old* friend of yours, in any case. Isn't that so?'

'That has nothing whatever to do with the topic under discussion,' said Rennie evasively.

But it *had*, hadn't it? she thought unhappily. Rennie *plus* Magda. Rennie *minus* Magda. What was it to be? Whichever it was, it made all the difference in the world so far as Keith was concerned!

It made a difference to Rennie, too. The difference between a full, happy heart, and an empty, lonely one. She must put that fact right out of her mind just now, however. Whatever decision she came to in the end, she must act in Magda's best interests, this much she was quite determined upon.

'Cheer up!' chided a deep voice above her, breaking into her preoccupation. 'You can always write.'

'Write?'

'Write a letter. To the *old* pilot friend. We do have mail deliveries out here, you know! What's his other name, by the way? Keith—?'

'Stamford.' Rennie turned away abruptly, seeking a change of subject. 'Where has Magda gone? She has disappeared.'

'I sent her to find Elspeth. She'll be in the kitchen.'

'Who is Elspeth?'

'Elspeth Brodie, my housekeeper. One of those *friends* whose existence you doubted,' he told her a little grimly. 'Apart from Elspeth, the two lubras who help her – Nellie and Mayra – will be in the kitchen just now, and Ashley Ryarton will be in for lunch. Ash is our book-keeper – and storeman, too, of course. The others won't be in till sundown, and as they eat down at the quarters, you may not meet them until tomorrow.'

So there were other people here, after all!

'Who are the others?' she asked curiously.

'The rest of those friends, Renata. All the people who help to make Barrindilloo the efficient property which it is. Jackeroos, station-hands, the aboriginal stockmen – and Murtie you've already met. You and Magda will get to know each one of them in a surprisingly short time, you'll find. The people of the Outback are noted for their friendly disposition.'

All the people of the Outback *except* the Boss of Barrindilloo, thought Rennie, somewhat bleakly.

There was no doubting his chilly tone, although he preserved a carefully impassive face along with it. Why she should mind, she just did not know. After all, one could not, and should not, expect one's enemies to be friendly, should one? Civility was the most one could expect, and that was precisely what Rennie was receiving right now. Cool, careful civility. Therefore she had no good reason to experience this strange feeling of hurt and rebuff!

Chad was right, as it turned out.

In the next few weeks, she and Magda got to know everyone on the property – or at least the people in and around the homestead. Chad had found it necessary to explain that there were others at the several out-stations whom she perhaps would not meet at all in her brief sojourn at Barrindilloo, unless they happened to ride in to the homestead block for supplies. There were also boundary-riders, well-sinkers, drovers, horsebreakers, prospectors, bagmen, moving about out there in that vast tract of lonely country, seemingly absorbed in the isolated existence which they had chosen to pursue, either working for the station bosses as they travelled from one property to another, or for themselves in the hope of 'striking it lucky', depending upon what they had chosen to do in life.

Nearer home, there were the station hands, and Murtie; also four young jackeroos who were a year or two younger than Rennie herself. They spent a good deal of their off-duty time in entertaining Magda, who no doubt amused them in return with her citified remarks and quaint observations.

The aboriginal stockmen did not live in the weather-board buildings where the station hands and jackeroos were. They preferred to have their own settlement, down on the creek. When Rennie and Magda walked in that direction, they could see their dwellings – a huddle of tin-sheeted wurleys amongst the sprinkling of gums and tall paper-barks, where wispy rags of clothing were strung out on wires amongst the branches of the trees, and strange, fatty smells emanated from the smouldering ashes of the fire nearby. Bulging-tummied, wiry dark-skinned children played in the shade at the water's edge, while the ubiquitous camp dogs watched half-heartedly, or nosed around with disconsolate curiosity amongst the bones and litter beyond the camp's immediate vicinity in the hope of unearthing a decaying morsel of food.

It seemed to Rennie that there were almost as many dogs as there were piccaninnies. When she remarked on this one day to Ashley, the book-keeper, he laughed heartily.

'Possibly you're right, Rennie. I haven't taken a count lately, so I can't tell you for sure.'

Rennie and Ashley had become firm friends. There was something inherently gentlemanly about this shy, humble, sixtyish man who had been quite prepared to accept Rennie without attempting to judge her in the way that Chad did. From Ashley she did not receive those long, speculative looks, those snide remarks which suggested that she was a – a frivolous, insincere sort of person, following an equally frivolous and shallow career.

74

Well, if that was how Chad Sandasen saw her, why should she worry? His good opinion was of no interest to her!

'What do they want them all for?' she asked now, intrigued.

Ashley shrugged. He was sitting in his office with a couple of files and a leather-bound ledger in front of him, plus the tray of tea and scones which Rennie had offered to bring for Elspeth for his morning smoko. She had added an extra cup for herself, and was now perched on a corner of Ash's flat-topped desk, an unconsciously lovely figure in a sleeveless yellow shift and thonged sandals that wound, criss-cross fashion, up her slender, bare brown legs, to calf level.

'It's just that those dogs are *there*, and always have been, I reckon.' Ash wrinkled his nose consideringly. 'They don't need them for hunting now, the way they used to, because they get plenty of station tucker, and number one tucker at that – generous rations of tea, flour, sugar, and meat. Very few of those station stockmen are of absolutely pure aboriginal blood any more, you see, Rennie. They've become admixed, over the years, with all the people who opened up their country to modern development – the white pioneer, the squatter, the Afghan camel-driver, the drover, the Chinese station-cook – and these outside influences have in some instances produced an unhappy sort of "half-way" status in society, which creates its own difficulties for them. In places they have been maligned and exploited, I'm afraid, but they are intelligent people basically. They possess an instinctive animal sense which makes them natural stockmen – some of the best in the world – for which men like Chad are sensible enough to have a great respect. Old Harry Goola out there is of almost pure descent, and his sons are skilled trackers, wonderful horsemen, grand stockmen. Chad often takes Harry to the places further north at musters, because Harry's very good at sitting there in Chad's helicopter, instructing the horsemen on the ground with his two-way radio just where to look for the strays, because otherwise they could be riding blind up and down gullies all day, wasting a lot of precious time. Harry took to the air like a duck to water, believe it or not. Chad often teases him about it, and calls him a "properfella chopper king, eh, Harry", and Harry in his turn is proud to think that he has mastered modern methods so readily. Chad thinks the world of him, and he of Chad. I reckon they'd do *anything* for Chad, Rennie. And in return for their loyalty and love, he looks after their every need, and helps them to manage their finances, too. They each get their "finger money" out of their wage, and then I bank the rest for them in a savings account, which gives them financial security. It's a thing they don't really understand very well, because it's their way of *life* which counts with them, above everything else, and beyond buying gay shirts and hair-oil and a few knick-knacks, they aren't tempted to spend money in the way that we might choose. If they want things, they ask Chad what he thinks.'

From her perch on the side of the desk, Rennie stretched out one leg and eyed her painted toes critically.

She had no wish to talk about Chad.

For no particular reason, the mere thought of him caused a painful tightening within her. When in his company, she felt even more uncomfortable than when she was just thinking about him. With his physical presence, the feeling almost always seemed to intensify alarmingly, and that was why Rennie spent her time in keeping out of his way!

'I think we counted eleven dogs down there, Magda and I,' she told Ash now, reverting quickly to their former topic of conversation.

'Quite likely. And a motley collection they are, I grant you.' He grinned. 'They're useful as blankets, if nothing else, I dare say.'

'Blankets?'

'Yes. Bed-cover,' elucidated Ash, amused at her dubious expression. 'Imagine yourself a round-tummied, skinny-limbed little piccaninny, curled up on a cold bright night between two warm, wire-coated, adoring

76

canines, and you have the picture, Rennie.'

'Oh, I see.' She glanced at him suspiciously, but he did not appear to be joking. 'No gammon?'

'No gammon.' He chuckled. 'You mightn't believe it, but I can assure you it can get very cold indeed out there in the middle of the night. Inland in a continent of this size, the temperature drops suddenly and sharply, from one extreme to the other. In places, it's so sudden that even the rocks start cracking and chipping under the strain of trying to adjust. I've a pile of nice grey blankets in that store for Harry and his kin whenever they want them, but they seem to actually *prefer* a dog or two thrown in with the bedding for good measure.' He replaced his cup on the tray. 'Thanks, Rennie. That was really beaut.'

Rennie beamed. '*I* made the scones this morning, Ash,' she confessed, flushing with pride at his unwitting compliment.

'You did, Rennie?' His bushy brows rose in surprise. 'I'd no idea that you were such an accomplished cook as that! You look much too decorative to be useful, do you know that?'

She laughed, pleased at his commending tone.

'Don't be silly, scones are easy compared with a lot of those lovely things that Elspeth turns out so beautifully.'

'Are they? I'm afraid I wouldn't know,' he grinned. 'But talking of Elspeth, I'm surprised that she's allowed you to take over in her domain. She guards that kitchen jealously, or always has done, up till now. Even Nellie and Mayra only go in at certain times, you know, because Elspeth has always insisted on doing all the cooking and baking herself.'

'I know. But she and I have reached a – well, a sort of understanding,' Rennie informed him proudly. 'We're friends, Elspeth and I. And she's been so kind to me, Ash. Since Chad keeps insisting that I drop into the background more and more, to allow Magda the opportunity of getting to know you all, so that she will gradually transfer her dependence from me to all the people here at

Barrindilloo, I – well, I sometimes find myself at a loose end. Sort of shut out. Elspeth knows how I feel, and she gives me things to do, you see.'

She had difficulty in hiding from Ash the hurt which she felt at the present state of things.

Magda was being drawn away from her relentlessly, ruthlessly, it seemed to Rennie. Already, Chad had succeeded in cultivating a close relationship with the little girl. He took her with him whenever he could.

It was a commonplace occurrence, now, to see the small, cotton-clad figure in her pretty beach-hat, perched on the back of the jeep as Chad bounced away in that shabby vehicle on some errand or another, or seated in front of his saddle on the handsome quarter-horse stallion he rode.

Each day Magda became browner and more blooming, her limbs firmer and rounder, the scars on her cheeks fading and healing, blending with her newly acquired tan just as Chad had predicted they would. And each day took Magda further away from Rennie. *She* wasn't invited on those outdoor excursions shared with such evident happiness by the small, talkative child and the tall, silent man.

Maybe Chad *wasn't* silent with Magda, though, like he was with Rennie. He couldn't be, in fact, or the little girl would not now possess this fund of information on all sorts of surprising things of which Rennie herself remained ignorant.

Magda had already learned a lot. She had learned, for instance, that the small furry brushtail possums which stole out at night to feed on leaves and insects, and swung cheekily upside-down by their prehensile tails, differed from their American opossum brothers because of their webbed feet and long 'great toe', which they were able to use almost like a human thumb. She knew that the Ringtails had two thumbs instead of one, which they could oppose to their three other fingers, rendering them incredibly dexterous as they climbed and gripped and pulled at the succulent gum-tips, stuffing them voraciously into their ever-greedy little mouths. She knew that the red kangaroos were more numerous than their great grey cousins; that the wallabies were squat and stunted by comparison, and ventured seldom from their timbered haunts in the scrub to feed on the open plains, as did the old-man kangaroo and his mate. She could identify the plaintive call of the swans that flew by night to new feeding grounds; the owl that cried 'Mo-poke' so mournfully from his home in the hollow tree near Harry Goola's settlement at the creek; the screech of the sulphur-crested cockatoos and the wondrously delicately-tinted Major Mitchells; the chittering of the rainbow-coloured finches and parakeets. She knew the river red-gum with its substantial, mottled bole; the scrawny mulga with its sea of yellow blooms; the water-loving paper-bark and the hardy ironbark; the sickly damp of the gidyea, the eerie drama of the ghost-gum; the beefwood, the bloodwood, the myall and wilga and desert oak. She had seen a frilled lizard with his ungainly Elizabethan collar raised in agitation, his mouth open in alarm, as Chad pointed him out; and several species of goanna (and *none* of them walked on their tails, Magda had assured Rennie earnestly, in response to her timorous inquiry!)

Magda had sat with Chad on the bank at the waterhole as the birds clamoured for roosts in the surrounding trees each evening – great flocks of duck and coot, egret and swan; watched the bustling of the water-hens and the gliding of the darters, the shuffling of the soft-hued pink and grey galahs as they vied for positions on the twisted, overhanging branches; suffered the inquisitive scrutiny of a pair of crested pigeons which came each night to the pepper-trees nearby. She had witnessed the manoeuvres of the sociable, ungainly pelicans as they cunningly joined ranks to ensnare a shoal of fish, invisible to the human eye beneath the dark green water; had marvelled at the patient stance of the heron that stood, enshrined in its graceful solitude, at the pool's edge.

Chad had shown her an eagle's nest in the tangle of stunted mulga on the plains, and the tiny, matted abodes of the marsupial mice tucked away in the grasses.

Chad had shown Magda *lots* of things. But not Rennie.

To Rennie, he remained courteously detached, unquestionably aloof.

She should have been thankful, she told herself vexedly, especially as she didn't care for that loose-limbed, easygoing country type, in any case. But for some odd reason, she wasn't thankful at all. In an attempt at self-honesty, Rennie asked herself now if her irritability over Chad's imperviousness was not because she was, and always had been, accustomed to arousing interest and admiring glances from the male of the species? Chad wasn't interested. Chad did not admire. Chad *ignored* – and ignored in a way that only Chad Sandasen *could* ignore! He ignored with a completeness that was total in its belittling and humiliating effect upon Rennie, and the realization made her so angry that she had now decided to ignore him in her turn. It was the only means of retaliation at Rennie's disposal, stuck away out here on a lonely cattle station, surrounded by all Chad's faithful and devoted minions, to whom it would have been folly to utter one word of criticism of their beloved Boss.

Rennie suspected – *more* than suspected, she *knew* – that Chad did not even notice her ignoring him! Beyond giving her the instructions he expected her to follow in relation to Magda's everyday routine at Barrindilloo, he had left it to the rest of his staff to make friendly overtures to the girl who had brought the child all this way at his behest. And Rennie, who had clearly made a very great sacrifice to do this very thing, felt rebuffed.

Yes, however illogically, she felt *rebuffed!*

Surely a man of Chalford Sandasen's business acumen must realize that, other considerations apart, her career had suffered already because of her enforced absence. A top model couldn't just disappear 'down-under' for months on end, and expect to resume where she had left off at the end of that period of absence, just as though nothing had happened. He might at least have shown that he appreciated the gesture for the magnanimous one that it was! Could he not have relaxed his chill, formal approach just the tiniest bit, to let her know that her own unselfish interest in Magda's welfare had been recognized, and even applauded? Could he not have shown her just *one* little marsupial mouse in its little grass home, or that eagle's nest out there in the mulga? No, it seemed that he could not, so the best thing to do was to maintain the same stiff aloofness as he did himself.

Rennie found herself more than naturally grateful for the friendliness of all those other station people – of the light-hearted jackeroos, the laconic station-hands, the admiringly helpful Murtie, the grinning Harry Goola who referred to her as 'that youngfella missus', the plump and amiable Elspeth, the giggling Mayra and the doe-eyed Nellie, and most of all Ashley Ryarton himself, always so patient and informative, accepting and understanding.

Ash had told Rennie, at the very beginning of their friendship, quite a lot of things about himself that she might otherwise never have guessed. Today, it came as a surprise to learn that Ash was a widower – a 'family' man, a grandfather, in fact! – and that his children were all married, two sons living in other States, and a daughter in the city.

'I went down there myself for a while,' he confessed to Rennie, 'to the Big Smoke. That was after I lost my wife. Before that, we had always lived at Koontilla – that's another of the Sandasen stations, farther north. After Eileen went, I just couldn't stay there, somehow. There were too many reminders of her, everywhere I looked or turned. I thought my sense of loss would never grow less, so long as I stayed there, so I went away. To the city – Sydney. That's where my daughter is, you see. We were always very close, she and I.'

'But you didn't stay.' Rennie gazed curiously at the weathered, grey-haired, kindly man – at Ash, her friend.

He shook his head. A small smile hovered at the corner of his mouth, a smile of self-derision, half-amused, a little regretful.

'I couldn't,' he stated simply.

'You couldn't?'

'No, Rennie, I couldn't.' He shrugged, spread his fingers ruefully. 'I wanted to, but I couldn't. I just couldn't stick it, not for very long.'

'But why not, Ash?' Rennie thought of that big, excitingly turbulent city, with its arched bridge and newly-flowering Opera House, its pulsing night-spots, its fabulous harbour, those marvellous beaches frilling right up and down the entire coast. 'Why not?'

'I guess I was homesick, Rennie.' The big, thick-set man looked faintly ashamed of this admission, but he met her eyes honestly. 'Yes, that's all that's to it, it was as simple as that. I was homesick. Homesick for the bush.'

'For the *bush*?' She was incredulous. What could the bush have to offer by comparison?

'Yes, for the bush.' Ash's expression gentled suddenly, and his mouth was smiling again, not even faintly ashamed this time. 'I was homesick for the bush, Rennie – for the "great Outback". It kept calling me and calling me. I longed for the open heavens overhead, with their milky spill of stars winking down on me at night; for the scent of the mulga, the warm wind off the plains, the sting of sand against my cheeks, the cloying of dust in my throat; the still, peculiar hush at noon, when the whole world seems to be temporarily suspended in timeless peace; for the screeching of birds going over at sundown, and those tentative first stirrings of the bush world at dawn – oh, and many, many other things besides, Rennie. Things that steal up on you unawares, and wrap themselves around your heart so secretly and skilfully that you aren't even properly aware that they are there at all. You only miss them when they *aren't* there, if you know what I mean?'

She nodded. 'I think I can understand a little bit, Ash.'

Someone else had said almost the same thing as Ash, hadn't he? Someone more articulate, but it amounted to the same thing in the end, didn't it, even though the 'someone else' had expressed it a little bit differently? Rennie could even now recall the glow in those keen green eyes, the tender softening of Chad's forbidding mouth, the deepening affection in his voice as his fingers had gone on stroking the nape of her neck all the time he was speaking of the selfsame thing as Ash, telling her of the spell of the Outback which, once experienced, lingered for ever, enmeshing people in its magic and wonder and vastness, so that they never wanted to leave, always longed to return.

> ' – And I crossed again,
> Over the miles of saltbush plain.
> The shining plain that is said to be
> The dried-up bed of an inland sea.'

Rennie didn't want to remember the way Chad had spoken those words. She wished that she could forget. She'd have liked to forget, too, the touch of those strong brown fingers as they ran over her own smooth, golden skin, the warmth of his breath against her brow, the odd gleam in those strangely penetrating green eyes as Chad had tilted her chin and studied her tear-stained face with such a disconcertingly thoughtful expression.

She *wanted* to forget, but she couldn't.

In bed that evening, the memory returned to haunt her, as it so often did. How stupidly weak she had been to allow herself to break down in front of that man! If only she hadn't, there'd be nothing to remember, nothing to tease her mind when all she longed for was to go to sleep.

Rennie tossed restlessly beneath the sheet, too disturbed to rest. At piccaninny daylight she got up and stole out on to the veranda, pulling her light silk kimono about her, glad of the coolness of the smooth pine boards against the soles of her bare feet. She peered beyond the gauze, then eased the swing-door open softly, and slipped out into the mild air of the false dawn, to sit on the step, her chin cupped in her palm as she strove to sort out the confusion in her mind.

If only Keith were here, she thought with sudden longing. If only Keith were here, *he* would put everything into its proper perspective. Keith had a way of laughing off doubts, of shrugging away complications as though they did not exist. Keith was single-minded, refreshingly so. If he had been here now, he would have made Rennie laugh with some idiotic and ridiculously irrelevant remark, and then he'd have kissed her, in that exciting, possessive way that sent the blood rushing to Rennie's head and drove all doubts and fears from her brain.

Ah, Keith! Where are you at this very moment, I wonder?

Rennie raised her eyes to the paling sky where the stars were fast disappearing, snuffing out their tiny, winking lights one by one, turned as a footfall sounded on the veranda above her and the door opened quietly.

Chad Sandasen stood at the top of the steps for a moment, and then came down them to her side.

CHAPTER FIVE

'RENATA? You startled me, sitting there at this hour of the morning! Are you all right?'

He glanced at her keenly in the grey light before hitching his moleskins and taking the opposite coping stone to the one upon which she herself was perched. His elastic-sided boots, with their defined stockman's heel, gleamed in the dimness, unsullied yet by the day's dust. His hair was sleek against his head, still darkly wet from the shower, and the unfamiliar tang of shaving lotion reached her nostrils as he leaned towards her.

'Couldn't you sleep?'

'Are you always up as early as this?' she countered, wishing he would cease that probing inspection.

'Round about now, yes, give or take a few minutes.' The wide shoulders shrugged. 'It's the first time I've run into *you*, though. What's the matter? Are you still worrying about Magda? If so, you needn't. It seems to me that she is settling down admirably, even better than I had dared to hope.'

'I was thinking about *myself*,' Rennie told him reprovingly.

Magda, Magda. It was always the child with Chad, just as though Rennie did not exist, or if she did exist, was not worthy of the least consideration.

'Yes?' A grin hovered at one corner of the level mouth. 'From your mooning expression just now, I'd have said you might even be thinking about the boy-friend?'

'Him, too,' admitted Rennie defiantly, nettled at the accuracy of his perception. 'And why shouldn't I be thinking about Keith?'

'No reason at all, except that the process hardly appears to bring pleasure or happiness in its wake.' A pause. 'I can see that you are fretting here, but I'm going to have to ask you to be patient for a while longer, I'm afraid, Renata. Although Magda is becoming well accustomed to her new way of life, I don't think she's ready yet to have you walk right out of it. Until that time comes, your presence here is a necessity. After that—' again the shrug – 'you will be free to resume that other life where you left off, since it appears to hold such irresistible charms for you.'

Rennie pressed her lips together. 'You think me frivolous, don't you, Chad? Frivolous and insincere? Funseeking, shallow?' She swallowed, to conceal the tremor of real hurt in her voice.

'Have I ever said that?' He shook his head. 'I have told you already. I think you're misguided rather than insincere, Renata. In any case, does it really matter to you what I think?'

She bit her lip.

'Of course not. It's quite immaterial, so far as I'm concerned. It's just that – that – one doesn't like to be judged – or rather, *mis*judged. I have felt that you have done that from the very beginning.'

'You forget that I found out a lot about you before we met, I think. I got the background fairly accurately.'

Her colour rose.

'You spied!' she accused him, aggrieved. 'How did you do it, Chad? A detective agency or something? In any case, it was despicable!'

He raised an eyebrow at her vehemence.

'Why get so het-up, if you reckon your way of life is above reproach? It was *Magda*'s life I was concerned about, may I remind you, Renata, and not your own. And what I learned about it – the inquiries were made through my wool firm, by the way, and not through a detective agency in the dramatically underhand way you seem to think! – what I learned was sufficient to tell me that Magda stood very little chance of turning out any better than her mother, under the circumstances, and the remedy appeared to lie with me.'

'Her mother? Betty? Why, she was my own cousin!'

'I know. And you cannot deny that she was quite unfit to be a parent in the first place. Unstable, scatterbrained – a model, too, like yourself, when Neil met her, I believe?'

86

'She was also lovable, generous—'

'To a fault. She went through Neil's money like water.'

'That's true, I admit, and her own savings, too. They went through it together. They *lived*. They were *happy*.'

'I'd prefer to call it irresponsible.' His mouth had become grim.

'But you can't blame Betty alone for that!' Rennie was indignant. 'What about Neil's part in it? What about your own brother?'

'She was older than he, by several years, wasn't she? *She* should have known better – especially after the child came. What Neil needed was a steadying influence. If he had to make a marriage while he was still so patently immature, why couldn't it have been to someone else, to someone stable, sensible, home-loving? *Maternal*, if you like?' he queried coldly, and there seemed to Rennie a wealth of bitterness behind that question.

Chad Sandasen had obviously loved his wild young brother with a depth of feeling that Rennie would hardly have believed possible in the stern, grim-faced man at her side. He had loved him, hoped that some day Neil would get his adventuring out of his system, return and settle down, take his place in the pastoral scene, eventually make his own personal contribution to the welfare of his family, to all those properties, to the nation itself, in the way that Sandasens had always done. He must have been disappointed when he had heard of Neil's marriage, she could understand his reaction, in a way. A model, and older than he, at that! A hurried, furtive, register-office affair. No, not furtive, *never* furtive. Whatever Neil had been, he had never been capable of pretence. It was just that he was carefree, careless, couldn't be bothered with all the frills. 'Darling, let's surprise them,' he'd said impatiently, and Betty, adoring him, had agreed. And after that the money ran out, and Chad wouldn't let him have any more, and Magda arrived, and there were all those jobs, one after the other, and then – the fatal car-crash. But they had been happy. *Happy.*

'They were *happy*,' she told Chad fiercely, in a choking

87

voice. 'Isn't that enough? To be happy? Shouldn't you be able to forgive all the rest, forget all the shortcomings, because of the fact that they made each other happy? Who are you to judge? They loved each other, can't you understand? No, perhaps you wouldn't understand such a thing – the precious and wonderful thing it can be, true love between a man and a woman. The sort of love that shares and trusts and doesn't question, gives all for the sheer joy of giving, because it is given to the loved one. That sort of love is rare and wonderful. It transcends things like family approval, or money and position, or stability and security.'

She paused for breath, looked over at Chad, to find that he was already looking at her – very attentively, in that way he had which produced the familiar, uncomfortable feeling.

'And is that the sort of love that you yourself have experienced, Renata?' he asked now, gravely.

The sheer unexpectedness of what he had said brought Rennie's thoughts earthwards with an unpleasant bump. *Had* she experienced that sort of love? she asked herself uncertainly. With Keith?

Certainly Keith's kisses could send her into a sort of seventh heaven, there was no doubt about that. His compliments could make her glow with pleasure. One lingering look was sufficient to transport her with its hidden promise, could bring a thrill of tingling excitement to her by its very implications. Of course, she *had* been disappointed over his attitude regarding Magda, but surely the very fact that he *wasn't* prepared to share Rennie herself with anyone else must mean that his love for her was total, all-absorbing, just as hers was for him?

'Yes,' she said firmly, 'that is my own feeling exactly.' And she watched Chad's brown hands as they abruptly stopped twirling his broad-brimmed hat between his knees, and gripped the brim quite tightly instead. He always seemed to carry his hat with him, apparently, even at this early hour, although he hadn't actually got it on his head. 'Oh! Whatever is that?' she added, startled, as a sudden mad gale of laughter came ringing over the

88

ground from the direction of the river. It was a hysterical, chuckling sound, human almost, that rent the grey dawn air with noise, and set the dogs barking down at Harry Goola's gunyahs, and the cocks crowing in the fowlyard at the back of the house.

Good heavens! Somebody's mirth had got quite out of control! The laughter rose to an abandoned crescendo, as if unable to stop itself.

'Kookaburras,' Chad told her, standing up and clapping the hat on his brow forthwith. 'Or "laughing jackasses", as they're sometimes called. They do it every morning, Renata.' He smiled down at her, but there was still a hint of the former gravity lingering in his eyes. 'If they didn't laugh every morning like that, it would be a poor lookout for all of us. We'd have no day to look forward to.'

'How do you mean, Chad?'

Rennie stood up, too, and he frowned as he saw her bare feet.

'You shouldn't be out here like that, without even slippers. You could tread on something – a trapdoor spider, anything. Don't do it again, Renata.'

'I won't,' she assured him, obedient for once. 'Tell me about the kookaburras. Why wouldn't we have any day?'

'It's an old aboriginal belief,' he told her, taking her arm and guiding her firmly up the steps again and back to the veranda. 'One of their ancient Dreamtime legends. They believed, you see, that the sun is really a big fire, started up there each morning by the good spirits to bring light to the world. At first, the fire is only small and the flame weak, but by midday it becomes very hot and fierce. Then, by evening, it glows red in the dying embers of the sunset. The spirits felt they needed something to tell the world below that daylight had come, so they instructed the morning star to come out and shine as brightly as he could. The trouble was, nobody saw him, because they were still fast asleep. So the good spirits asked the kookaburras to laugh very loudly at each and every dawn-time, so that the people down on the ground would wake up and see that the fire was lit and day had begun. They've been doing it ever since, and that's why they're laughing right now, in fact.' Chad's voice was whimsical.

'What a lovely idea!' Rennie was intrigued.

'Lovely, so long as the kookaburra agrees to co-operate. If he didn't, the spirits would take the huff and refuse to light the fire any more, and we'd all have to be content with eternal twilight.'

'Do they really believe that?'

'They're a very superstitious people, Renata. There's a reason for everything in the aboriginal mind, even for the things we may take for granted, and they find their explanations as logical as we find them quaint. The piccaninnies aren't supposed to mimic the kookaburra, because it will bring bad luck. And if they do, legend has it that an extra tooth will grow on top of the others, to show that they've mocked the harbinger of dawn, and threatened the world with the possibility of darkness for ever.'

'What a load of responsibility for those poor kookaburras, then!' Rennie smiled at the mere idea. 'What are they like, Chad? To look at, I mean?'

'They're brown and white, quite big birds, with a strong beak that can snap up a frog or break a small snake's back at a single flip. They are the largest of the kingfisher tribe, in fact, Renata. I'm surprised you haven't seen one. You must get Magda to point one out for you,' he suggested quite kindly, before he went striding away into the dawn which those kookaburras had so recently laughed into existence; and Rennie, feeling curiously deflated, went back to her bed to wait for the kindly aboriginal spirits to get their sun-fire burning just a little bit more brightly, before she got up to face another day at Barrindilloo.

The morning passed uneventfully.

Nellie and Mayra giggled and chattered as they flitted about their household tasks, like a couple of gay budgerigars in the brightly-coloured cotton overalls which they wore. Later, they sat in the dappling of shade on the back veranda, peeling vegetables together for the next meal, while Elspeth took advantage of temporary peace in the kitchen region to bake some bread.

The appetizing, yeasty smell assailed Rennie's nostrils as she saw Magda safely installed at the transceiver-set for the school-of-the-air session, and walked out on to the side veranda beyond.

Already Magda had been twiddling the knobs as Rennie left her side, tuning herself in to receive her morning lessons from Base; she was able to deal with the complete routine all by herself now, calling up, answering her call-in sign, replying to the teacher's questions along with the other country pupils scattered throughout the vast interior of the Australian continent.

Each base covered a wide area, each call-sign represented a little lonely bush-pupil, who – because of this wonderful medium of cancelling those incredible distances – was lonely no longer! Instead, all the children had become part and parcel of one big school 'family', able to work and learn co-operatively, and to participate in the daily chatter that preceded the school session. This was known locally as the 'cockatoo', and corresponded to the adult free-for-all of airborne gossip, appropriately dubbed the 'galah session', after those garrulous parrots with their soft pink-and-grey plumage and their love of noisy interchange.

Magda's high treble, making her own eager contribution to the morning yabber, reached Rennie's ears as she went down the steps and walked somewhat aimlessly in the direction of the stockyards.

From there she could hear the sound of hammering, which meant that one or another of the men must be around. And that, in its turn, meant that Rennie herself might find someone with whom to talk. Elspeth would not welcome interruptions with her bread-making this morning, and Nellie and Mayra needed but the smallest pretext to stop work altogether when they were spoken to, standing together, leaning on their brooms with those dazzling white, wide smiles, or nudging each other with their skinny, dusky arms and dissolving into fits of giggles. Their domestic attacks on the house were sporadic enough, one felt, without contributing to their inefficiency, and yet they were a lovable, friendly pair who had already won a place in Rennie's reluctant heart. Who could resist those beaming black eyes, those wonderful water-melon grins?

The hammerer turned out to be Murtie. He was mending a slip-rail, sinking an old horseshoe into the strainer-post to form a slot, and as Rennie approached he put down the hammer, pushed back his hat, and wiped the beads of sweat from his wrinkled brow.

'G'day, Renata.'

The old man eyed the young woman before him with marked appreciation, took in the beautiful cut of putty-coloured linen shorts and shirt with their saddle-stitched pockets, the ridiculous proportions of Rennie's floppy, outsized beach-hat, the slender shapeliness of her long brown legs, and the sheer loveliness of that pale curtain of hair that fell straight about her shoulders. Even the way she removed her sun-glasses to smile at him before replacing them and climbing on to the top rail at his side held a certain fascination for Murtie, which he wasn't slow to show. There was an elegance about Renata's every action of which she seemed to be entirely unaware, and her smile just now had been almost hesitant, deprecating, as she said humbly,

'I hope I'm not interrupting you, Murtie, coming to watch like this?'

'Course you aren't, Renata! Haven't I told you often enough just ter come along ter Murtie if you're at a loose end, eh?' He wiped his bare forearm over his forehead again. 'By crikey, I could use a pint right now! This heat's a fair cow!'

'A pity there isn't a pub just around that corner.' Rennie smiled again, and waved desultorily in the general direction of the harness-shed.

'Maybe it's just as well there *isn't*,' he told her frankly. 'Reckon when I get on the beer, I like ter make it a decent bender, Renata — a dinkum *occasion*, like. That ole poet knew 'is onions when 'e said, "The track o' life is dry enough, an' crossed with many a rut; but oh! we'll find it rougher still when all the pubs is shut." I like me pubs, I must admit, now and then.'

He grinned, and his sun-seamed face went into a thousand wrinkles, his dark eyes, merry with fun, almost disappearing beneath his beetling brows.

How typical of Murtie to produce an appropriate verse at the drop of a hat, thought Rennie, amused. He was forever quoting his beloved 'poets', and had confessed to possessing only six books in his bachelor hut, all of them in verse. The selection included Shakespeare, and it was odd to hear snippets of *Hamlet* or *Richard the Second* rolling glibly off the tongue of this sagging-breeched, dusty-booted old Outbacker, repeated in his slow, nasal drawl which somehow yet managed to imbue each line with the dignity and expression it deserved.

'Reckon I never wanted any other books but them,' he had told her, slightly sheepishly. 'You get ter *know* them books like you was born with 'em. They get ter be your *mates*. When I finish the last one, I go back over 'em all again in turn, from start ter finish, an' it's just like meetin' an old friend.'

'Where *are* the pubs that you go to, when you do go for an – a – er – bender, Murtie?' asked Rennie now, settling herself more comfortably on the bleached fence-rail.

'Well, I'm not much of a one fer towns, and that's the truth, Renata. I might go once a year, maybe, an' then it's to Meridian.' He gave the horseshoe a final swat with the hammer, and then threw the tool back amongst its fellows in a greasy black bag at his feet. 'My next chance'll most likely be at our own race meetin', here at Barrindilloo, but it'll all depend on how me luck's holdin' out, whether I have a bit of a blinder or not, see. I'm not one o' them booze-artists who can't do without the stuff,' he was at pains to emphasize. 'If me bettin's goin' dead sweet, I'll probably just settle fer the odd pint or two. If she's crook, I'll maybe decide ter have a bit of a blinder with some of the boys. It depends,' he temporized.

'I didn't know you had a race meeting *here*, Murtie. When is it? Where do you hold it?'

'Barrindilloo has one o' the best race meetin's in the

land, I reckon, Renata. It might not be the biggest, but it's one o' the *best*,' he insisted with pride. 'Gen'lly we hold it just after The Cup, because we're still in the mood for a spot of hide-crackin', see. But this year, Chad put it off a month or two, seein' that you an' Magda was comin' just about that time. Reckon 'e thought 'e'd have enough on 'is plate gettin' Magda settled down first.'

'So when is it likely to be, and where do you have it?'

'Three weeks, maybe, from now. That's about the latest Chad'll chance it before the weather might break. We hold it in the same place every year, about fifteen mile from the homestead, out at the Yogill Bore. We've got a permanent site out there, ablutions an' the lot, see. An' tents galore. Everybody camps, an' we cart out enough tucker an' booze for a two-day meetin'. The place is swarmin' with visitors, then, Renata, just as busy as Pitt Street, I reckon. They come from all over – the cities, the other stations, the other States. All them girls—'

He picked up the tool-bag, shaking his head as he stooped once more to retrieve the two spare horseshoes which he had not used, and began to amble away in the direction of the blacksmith's shop.

'What girls?' asked Rennie attentively, finding that she had to hurry to keep up, in spite of Murtie's advanced years and slightly rheumatic gait.

'All them city sheilas, they come swarmin' up here like bees to a sugarbag.' He placed the tool-kit carefully back on its shelf, turned, and grinned pensively. 'Reckon it's Chad they're after. 'E takes 'em out in the city, see, an' they think they've got it made, so they all come up here at race-time, ter see can they get the hobbles on 'im fer good, but so far 'e's given 'em the slip. Mind you, they don't sing *out* about why they've come. They bring an escort, or maybe a party of four or six, so they can pair off fer dancin' an' the like, but most of the eye-flutterin' is in Chad's direction, fer all that!'

'Are they very pretty, those girls?' Rennie wanted to know, and somehow found that she was almost holding her breath for the answer, just as though it really mattered.

94

'A proper eyeful, some of 'em,' Murtie told her with enthusiasm. 'But none of 'em will ever manage ter crack the stockwhip when Chad's around, yer can bet on that! 'E treats 'is women like 'e treats them horses 'e breaks in, I reckon, sort of careless-particular. 'E likes 'em with a bit of spirit, an' 'e enjoys tamin' them and bringin' them ter heel, but 'e hasn't ever picked one out fer keeps, Renata, not *yet*.'

The arrogant brute, thought Rennie waspishly. She could just imagine him playing those lovely, hopeful girls fast and loose, stringing them along with that casually charming manner he could adopt, when all the time it was just a game to him. Serve him right if he got his fingers burnt one day, and one of those pretty creatures succeeded in shattering that marble heart of his right into a thousand wounded little pieces!

Worry began to niggle inside her again. Worry for Magda.

What if Chad *never* took a wife, not *ever*? What if he went on through life, playing around with those lovely girls without ever settling down to marriage at all? That would mean that Magda would only have Elspeth and Nellie and Mayra. No proper mother-figure at all, really, to take the place of the one she had lost, and the one whom Rennie herself had now, in part, become.

She sighed. It was difficult to know what to do for the best, it really was!

Just lately Rennie had begun to admit, with silent reluctance, that Magda had blossomed and thriven in this country atmosphere. She had acquired a new poise and self-confidence, evident in the assured way in which she now manipulated the transceiver-set, participated so enthusiastically in the morning programme, laughed and joked with the jackeroos and station hands, shadowing Chad with determined devotion whenever possible, but reverting willingly enough to the company of Elspeth and the others when he wasn't there.

The homestead routine was pleasantly varied, interesting enough to keep the child preoccupied, repetitive enough to impart a feeling of security. Each morning, the

School of the Air. Each afternoon, correspondence lessons which were sent out in the mail and returned when completed, and which Rennie herself usually supervised in a happy, relaxed atmosphere at one corner of the veranda. In between times, there were heaps of exciting outdoor occupations with Chad – those activities in which Rennie herself had never been invited to share – fishing, swimming, picnicking, bird-watching, and lately, riding a small, quiet chestnut pony which Chad had had brought over, especially for Magda, from one of his other places.

Rennie felt genuine pangs of jealousy as she watched Chad giving Magda her riding lessons from her unseen vantage point on the lawn beyond the shrubbery.

Not that Rennie was envious of the lessons. She didn't need *those*. It was the riding itself which she coveted!

Rennie loved horse-riding. She was an accomplished equestrienne, in fact – had ridden to hounds back in England on various occasions, and seldom missed the White City Trials, if she could help it.

And here she was, having to stand here, forlornly watching her favourite occupation in progress down there at the yards, knowing quite well that she would not be welcomed if she went one step further than this spot on the lawn, from where she had a clear view of Chad's tall, sunburnt figure, in the tight, faded moleskins, wide hat and dusty boots, putting the small pupil through her paces again and again with patient and characteristic thoroughness.

He hadn't invited Rennie. And he wasn't likely to!

And even if he *had*, she had left her hacking-jacket and breeches, her polished boots and hard-topped hat, back there in the flat in London. To Rennie it was as important to *look* nice as it was to ride correctly – part of her professional pride and training, she supposed – and all she had with her here was a pair of denim jeans, which she had thought might be handy on the beach on a windy day, or for yachting, perhaps, in the inky, sunlit water of Sydney Harbour.

She sighed once more, as she followed Murtie out of

the gloom of the blacksmith's shop and into the hot sunlight, pulled up short behind him as a figure on horseback
came into sight around the side of the distant shearing-
shed.

'Look, Murtie! Who can it be?'

Rennie pointed excitedly. One did not expect to see a
complete stranger appear out of nowhere, out here in a
lonely and remote place such as Barrindilloo.

This particular stranger was a girl – a very, very
beautiful girl, at that – and she seemed to know exactly
where she was going. She couldn't be a stranger after all,
even though Rennie herself had never seen her before.

Murtie put back his head so that the angle of the brim
of his battered felt shaded his eyes from the glare, and
squinted at the far-off, approaching rider.

'That'll be Leith Mindon,' he told her, chuckling. 'One
o' them sheilas that'd like ter hobble Chad fer keeps. She's
a good sort, though, Leith. If I was layin' bets, she'd be
odds-on favourite.'

'Oh.' Rennie, in her turn, screwed up her eyes and
viewed the approach of the newcomer with increased
interest.

'Her an' 'er dad'll be out at the outstation next ter Barrindilloo,' Murtie vouchsafed. 'Often, when they're as
near as that, Leith'll borrow one o' the spares an' ride
over on the off-chance of havin' a yarn with Chad. 'Ullo
there, Leith! How's tricks?'

'Not so bad, Murtie. And you?'

The girl drew her horse to a standstill beside them, and
leaned forward to pat the animal's sweat-roughed neck.

She was a slim, well-proportioned girl, with short-crop-
ped, deep auburn curls, an entrancingly tilted nose, and
attractively spaced eyes a shade darker than Rennie's own
sherry-coloured ones. The curls clustered damply at the
nape of her slender neck as she removed the pith helmet
with its green fly-veil, and Rennie couldn't help noticing
that the hand which now held the topee against the
rider's knee was small, well-kept, with nicely shaped and
manicured nails, adorned with glistening coral-pearl varnish.

A pretty girl, no doubt about it – and feminine, every inch of her, right down to those shining coral fingertips.

Leith swung down to the ground in a single graceful movement, and smiled in a friendly way at Rennie.

'You must be the girl who brought Neil's daughter home from England,' she said, eyeing Rennie with unconcealed curiosity. 'I couldn't resist riding over to have a look at you when I found myself so near. We've all been dying to meet you, and to see Magda, too. After all, it takes a pretty earth-shaking event to make Chad postpone his race meeting, and that's just what he did when he heard you two were arriving round about that time.'

'Funny, we was just talkin' about that, Renata and me, at the very split second you came around the woolshed, Leith. I was tellin' Renata it'll probably be three weeks termorrer. You'll be there, of course?'

'Of course, Murtie,' agreed Leith, as though that were a foregone conclusion, which indeed it probably was! 'And it *is* to be in three weeks' time, because Chad called up to tell me so the other evening. Is he about, by any chance?'

Murtie scratched his chin.

'Reckon you ain't goin' ter be in luck today, Leith. I saw Chad ridin' out around sun-up with 'is tucker-bag and pint-pot aboard. There's no sayin' when 'e'll be back.'

'It doesn't matter, anyway,' replied Leith equably. 'It was really Renata and Magda I came over to see. I'll go up to the homestead and beg some lunch from Elspeth, if you'll be kind enough to invite me, Renata? Be a dear and take Blinker for me, will you, Murt? He's a slow old bag of bones, but he was the only spare available this morning.'

She relinquished her bridle to the waiting Murtie, and turned towards the homestead, and Rennie walked along by her side, reflecting that she and Chad must know and like each other very well, if he went to the bother of calling her up in the evening, when he came in so hot and tired and dusty after a heavy day out on the property.

'Did you have a good trip out?' Leith asked politely, then added, 'We've all been hoping that you might have come in on the galah session to tell us about it, Renata, but you never have.'

Rennie blushed. 'I haven't bothered to learn how to work the set, Leith,' she admitted candidly. 'I shall be here such a relatively short time, you see, that I don't suppose Chad thought it worth even demonstrating, although he taught Magda how to do it straight away. In any case, I'd be too shy to join in.'

'Nonsense!' stated Leith briskly. 'It's all very informal. We've been itching to hear you, and that English voice is quite charming. It would really take a trick. Just wait till I tell the others that I've actually *met* you. That will be a meaty piece of news for them! I must say—' she looked Rennie over appraisingly – 'Chad didn't tell us that you were quite so decorative.'

'Didn't he?' Rennie shrugged. 'I'm not a decorative person, really, Leith – not like *that*. I mean, it's just that I'm a model, professionally trained to make the best of myself,' she explained uncomfortably.

The other girl laughed openly at her embarrassment.

'My dear, it's nothing to *defend* yourself about. Besides, I've got eyes in my head, haven't I? Funny that Chad didn't mention it, though. He usually does, about anything out of the ordinary.'

Rennie's colour deepened.

She turned away, hoping that her companion would not notice. It would be humiliating to have to explain to this pretty, flame-headed creature that Chalford Sandasen had not bothered to mention it for the very same reason that Leith had unwittingly mentioned. So far as he was concerned, Rennie was obviously very ordinary indeed – so ordinary, in fact, that his green eyes passed over her carelessly and quickly in a cold, remote sort of way, and his mouth seldom lifted in that endearingly lopsided grin with which it responded to Magda, for instance, and his manner, although never lacking in actual courtesy, could scarcely be called warm or congenial.

Rennie hoped fervently that she would manage to

99

avoid the necessity of such an admission to anyone at all before she left Barrindilloo. She hardly liked to admit it, even to herself, because of the peculiar little ache it brought to the region of her heart. Hurt pride, no doubt, and she despised herself for it.

Now she spoke quickly.

'Tell me, do you live far away, Leith? How many miles did you ride this morning to get here?'

'Only about seven, actually. The outstation where our men are drafting just now is our nearest point to Barrindilloo. Our boundaries are conterminous as far as the Yogill Bore block, but the homesteads are over sixty miles apart. That's why I took the opportunity to come on, when my father was driving as far as that in the ute.'

'It's bad luck that Chad isn't here,' murmured Rennie awkwardly.

The distance this girl had come, just to see him, frankly appalled her. And riding all alone like that, on that dreadful horse!

'No matter, although of course it would have been nice to see him. As I said, the main object of my mission today was to meet you and Magda. Chad has already booked me for the race meeting, and that's scarcely any time away now, anyway.'

Leith had imparted this piece of information proudly.

Rennie supposed that by 'booked', she must mean that Chad had asked her to be his special girl-friend, his partner, over those two hectic days when all the people foregather from far and near to the Yogill Bore for the races and evening festivities. If that were the case, and what Murtie had just told her was also true, then there were going to be a lot of disappointed damsels at that meeting, and it was likely that all their 'eye-fluttering' would be in vain. Rennie could hardly imagine that any of them, even the city sophisticates, could possibly be more pretty or fetching than the girl who walked at her side right now!

They went up the steps, through the gauze door and on to the veranda.

'Magda?'

Leith hesitated, and surprisingly, Rennie realized that this pretty, confident girl was actually shy and awkward in the child's presence.

They talked for a while, and it was Rennie herself who glossed over the difficult silence, and set the small child laughing.

'Now, run and tell Elspeth that we've a visitor for lunch, will you, poppet? We shall need an extra place at the table, so you could ask Mayra or Nellie about that, too.'

Magda scampered off with alacrity, and Leith Mindon gave a tiny, wry grimace as she placed the topee on the cane table and sank into one of the veranda deck-chairs.

'I'm afraid children aren't my strong point,' she confessed ruefully to Rennie, as she accepted a tall glass of iced lemon squash which the other had brought from the fridge. 'I can't seem to strike quite the right note, ever – either treat them too young, so that they give me one of those dreadfully discomfiting oblique stares that only kids are capable of; or else endow them with an adult understanding that turns out simply not to be there – result, *more* horrid stares!' She sipped her drink thoughtfully. 'Just my luck, that Chad should choose to saddle himself with one, but I dare say it's something I can get used to in time, if I really try. With him there to help me, I'm sure it'll work out all right. Give me animals any day, all the same!'

Rennie did not quite know how to reply to this observation. She was fond enough of animals herself, but to prefer them to *Magda*—

Leith's implications had left her in no two minds about one thing, however, and that was that should Murtie wish to bet on this slender, chestnut-haired retroussé-nosed young woman as the successful candidate for the role of Mrs. Chalford Sandasen, it was more than probable that he would win!

Indeed, the way Leith had spoken, it looked as though a quite definite understanding had been reached. Rennie wasn't quite sure just how you reached that sort of understanding over an essentially public instrument like that transceiver-set appeared to be, but there was no doubt that Chad had achieved it, all the same. Perhaps he had written a letter, perhaps he had merely altered the tone of that deep voice of his in the speaking of some otherwise innocent phrase, or perhaps it had come about at some meeting quite a while ago, and was in fact a secret agreement of long standing between them.

However it had been accomplished, Leith had got the message, there was no question about that because of the decided way in which she had just spoken. And now she had passed the information on to Rennie, so that *she* had got the message, too!

At the sight of Ashley walking up from the store, Rennie rose to her feet.

'There's Ash. I'll just tell Elspeth that we're ready for lunch, if you'll excuse me, Leith. I'm sure you know where to go if you'd like a wash.'

It was a cheerful meal. Magda burbled on to Ash about her morning participation in the School of the Air, her initial wariness of the stranger in their midst forgotten in her eagerness to tell this man, of whom she had become so fond, about all that she had been doing so far today.

'And we sang "Green Grow the Rushes O", Ash. We've been learning it for days. I was given the bit about three, three, the rivals, and the others all got a line to learn, too. And today we put the whole thing together into a proper song. It was *great* fun, except that Philip out at Jabiru Ponds forgot his line, and for a minute there was just a lot of crackling and static and silence when Miss Brown called him in.'

'And what was Philip supposed to sing?' asked Ash, amused.

'He was "four for the gospel-makers". That's *easy*, but he forgot it, all the same. I didn't, though.'

'Good for you, Magda. Tell me, how is the pony coming along?'

'Oh, have you got a pony?' Leith was immediately interested.

'Yes, Chad got me one specially,' the little girl replied with some pride. 'Her name is Dolly, and I can trot her now.'

'I'd love to see her afterwards?'

'Well, you can if you like.' For some reason, Magda still sounded cautious.

After lunch was over, Ash went back to his store, and Rennie, Magda and Leith walked together over the hot, hard ground from the homestead to the stables, and while they were admiring Dolly, who should appear but Chad himself.

'Hullo, Leith. Where did you spring from? You must be working the Yogill Plains corner, are you?'

He had looked unsurprised, but pleased too, to see Leith Mindon leaning over the rail at Dolly's box.

'We are,' she nodded, 'so I just thought I'd ride over and meet Renata and Magda, when I had the chance.'

'Is that old nag in the horse-paddock yours, by any chance?'

Chad's white teeth gleamed for an instant in the darkness of his sun-browned face. His eyes, as they rested upon Leith's copper-bright, curly head, were smiling too.

'Yes, that's Blinker, all right. He was the only spare I could get hold of today.'

'Then that's a measure of how much you wanted to pay us a visit, and we should be flattered! Come, Leith, I'll ride back with you as far as the boundary. Your Blinker doesn't look the most dependable of mounts to me!'

It was with a tiny pang of something akin to envy that Rennie watched them leave the saddling yard a few minutes later, riding away out into the distance.

Leith sat erect, her helmet with its bobbing-cork fly-veil back in place. At her side, Chad's long, lean form looked broad and powerful, slanted easily in the saddle as his spirited stallion set the pace. He rode long-stirruped, the reins held loosely between the fingers of his left hand, while with his other he leaned down and opened the only gate they would have to go through, wheeling his horse and motioning his girl companion through. He did it with the same quiet gallantry as he so often did in holding open a door for old Elspeth, or even for Rennie herself, and the gesture somehow brought a lump to Rennie's throat.

The odd, choking feeling was still with her as she stood there, watching, until the man and the girl had ridden together right out of her vision.

CHAPTER SIX

THE tableau of those two riders remained with Rennie over the next couple of days, although she did her best to exorcise the memory from her mind.

Instead, she made herself think about other, more satisfactory things, such as the way in which Magda was progressing with her lessons, and the pleasantness of those interludes of chatting with Ash in his office, and Elspeth's warm gratitude over the many small acts by which Rennie found she was able to assist the older woman in the management of this sprawling homestead.

Her thoughts, too, dwelt longingly upon Keith. They dwelt *hopefully* now, as well as longingly, because it really did seem as though Magda was going to be happy at Barrindilloo after all. Admittedly there were drawbacks, such as Chad's bachelor state and the lack of company of other children in her own age group, but since her meeting with Leith Mindon, Rennie could well believe that the former would in due course solve itself. She was unable to bring herself to mention the lack of a wife to Chad – as she once had! – because she could imagine the way those green eyes would narrow so chillingly, the way that mobile mouth would immediately pull itself into the level, forbidding line that told her more clearly than words ever could to mind her own business.

She did, however, summon sufficient courage to broach the latter problem, and was surprised, when he replied, that she had not thought of such an obvious and suitable solution herself.

'When Magda is thirteen or fourteen I shall send her to a good boarding-school, where she will learn how to live with other girls, and how to participate physically in community life, in a way that she is able to do only mentally at the moment, by means of the radio communication with these other bush children, who are as isolated as she is herself. There's plenty of time to think about it, and in the meanwhile her personality can develop and emerge at its own pace. The lack of young companionship will not harm her temporarily. Indeed, it will give her time to get over her tragic experience. Time, too, for those scars to heal so that they are virtually invisible, and therefore unlikely to draw possibly hurtful comment from the others. Youngsters can be unintentionally tactless, not to say cruel, at times, Renata.'

'I hadn't thought of that aspect,' confessed Rennie with humility. Then – 'Where would you send her?'

'To one of the capitals. Possibly to Sydney itself. I have a sister in Brisbane, actually, who'd be only too willing to keep an eye on her, but the bulk of my business is transacted in Sydney.' He shrugged. 'I have to fly down often enough to be able to keep in constant touch with Magda and her progress. That's no problem at all.'

No, it wouldn't be a problem to Chad, Rennie could see that well enough. When he set his mind to doing something, he was surprisingly thorough and single-minded in the execution of that purpose.

A sudden warm excitement set her blood tingling, as she found herself imagining her *own* return to Sydney. To Keith. Free at last, in an *honourable* way, to go to him without encumbrances. She would miss her dear little Magda of course, but she could never give the child all the things which she now saw that Chalford Sandasen, the legal uncle, could and would give her.

Rennie could envisage the way Keith would hold his arms wide open so that she could fly right into them like a pigeon homing to its rightful nest. She could picture the way his eyes would linger so hungrily upon her, the way his lips would meet hers to claim her at last for his own.

She stood up abruptly, a little breathless, and as she left Chad's presence found herself submitting to a look so shrewd, so intent, that she wondered if he could possibly have guessed the turn of her own thoughts.

Soon – once she was quite, *quite* certain – Rennie would write to Keith and tell him all the things that were in her heart. She had been tempted to, many times, since she had come out to Barrindilloo, but had fought down the urge because of her sturdy resolution to put Magda's welfare first.

She had been unable initially to accept as more than the remotest possibility the idea that Chad Sandasen's way of life could be a favourable environment for her little orphaned charge. Because of the implications for herself and Keith, it was something that she *wanted* to believe, very much, almost more than anything else in the world. Indeed, the realization of how much it meant to her, personally, and to her whole future, acted as a curb upon Rennie's judgment. It was because she wanted so much that it should be so that she dared not be over-eager in telling herself that Chad and Barrindilloo were suitable substitutes for herself in caring for the child.

Now, she was almost convinced, and had allowed herself cautiously to recognize the fact.

The result was this sudden delicious feeling of anticipation and excitement on her own behalf – of sheer relief, as though an enormous burden of responsibility had removed itself from her slender shoulders, leaving her free at last to think, to dream, and to know that there was every likelihood of those same thoughts and dreams coming to fruition.

Rennie found herself humming lightheartedly as she strolled in the sunlit morning, over the lawn and beyond. She had no particular aim or purpose, but walked with a step that was today light and springy with hope and satisfaction, the outward testimony of her newly-acquired peace of mind. Her heart itself was singing this morning, a song of love that was soon to be requited. Love for Keith. A love that was to be reciprocated this time, because the verdict, the outcome, was not after all to be 'Rennie and Magda', it was to be 'Rennie alone'. She could go to Keith under his own terms, at last, and she would do that with a supreme gladness of heart.

And then it wouldn't even be 'Rennie *alone*'. It would be 'Rennie and Keith'. That phrase – 'Rennie and Keith' – she found inordinately satisfying. So satisfying that Rennie stopped her humming, and said it several times, experimentally, under her breath.

A cloud of dust at the high-railed stockyards caught her eye, and Rennie's steps turned carelessly in that direction.

As she approached, she could feel the reverberations of pounding hooves coming up through the ground to echo in the soles of her own feet, could hear the snorting and whinnying, and the sound of a voice that growled and shouted and coaxed by turns.

The voice belonged to Harry Goola. He was running a wild-eyed young colt around the yard on a long rein, pursuading it into obedience.

The animal's flank was shaggy with sweat, and Harry's own black face gleamed like wet satin, too, as he bent and turned with the horse, his filthy but ever-present pipe clenched unlit between his firm white teeth, as he pivoted on the spot where he stood while it circumscribed a widening, dust-trampled arc about him. Every now and then it would rear and plunge, cavorting away in a sudden fit of rebellion, and when it did that Harry would bite harder on his pipe, and dig the heels of his boots deeper into the powdery turf, winding the rope about his own wiry body, resisting and pulling until he regained control of the animal's actions.

As Rennie climbed up on to the rail she saw that there were some fifteen or twenty other horses shut in the adjoining yard to the one in which Harry was working.

They appeared to be of mixed ages and sizes, but all had one thing at least in common. They tossed their heads restlessly when Rennie looked down at them, snorted softly through dilated nostrils, wheeled in a body against the fence, and jostled from one end of their tight-packed prison to the other, as though realizing that soon they, too, must feel the pressure of that implacable rein, and the crack of the stockwhip perilously near their rump if they should choose to disobey its signals.

'What are you doing, Harry? Taming them?' asked Rennie, glad of the freedom her blue denim jeans afforded as she ascended agilely to the topmost rail.

'You-ai, missus. Harry bin break-in thatfella, allasame

him like-um more better get out there alonga that scrub.'
A grin. 'Him like-um more better prop'ly runaway
bush!'

Harry waved a black hand nonchalantly at the skyline
before bringing it to bear on the rope once more, and
grinned again, and Rennie found herself smiling readily
down into that wrinkled dusky face. With its glistening
black skin, short grey stubble of beard, broad nose, the
wide mouth with its ceremonial front gap between flashing
white teeth, and those wonderfully expressive liquid-
brown eyes, so clever and keen, alert even to the most
infinitesimal detail of object, sign or movement such as
the white man's eye could rarely perceive, Harry Goola
typified the best and finest characteristics of his aboriginal race. What was more, he had a personality to
match, a personality that was loaded with charm, dignity,
kindliness and merriment. At times the merriment took
control completely. At others, it was modified by the
superstitious overtones that were part of his inheritance,
and on those occasions, Harry's eyes could widen apprehensively, and his tongue would trip nervously over all
manner of gloomy prophecies and daunting predictions,
at such a speed that only Chad himself could understand.
But these moments were rare indeed. For the most part,
Harry was the happiest and sunniest of characters, a pic-
turesque figure in his faded shirt, straining braces, sagging, bagging trousers and ageing felt hat, with its oil-
stained crown and battered brim. The pipe completed
this picture. As Rennie had already observed times without number, Harry and his pipe were not to be parted, no
matter what he happened to be doing. That pipe was
as much a part of him as his spiky fuzz of grey
whiskers, his melting eyes, and his wide, white, gap-
toothed smile.

'Do you have to do that with them all?' Rennie asked
with interest, switching her gaze back to the unruly mob
in the adjoining yard.

'You-ai. Allabout,' agreed Harry unconcernedly.
'Harry bin break-in all that-one. Mebbe just twofella,
t'reefella not yet, missus.'

'Why do you put them all in together again, then? How do you know which are which?'

'Harry savvy allabout, missus, allasame that-one all prop'ly different, see. Some goodfella, some proper cheeky-fella, me work plenty longtime alonga that-one, savvy allabout, see.'

Rennie's eye scanned the horseflesh before her con-sideringly. She prided herself on being a fair judge, but had to admit that never before had she seen such a motley collection.

One powerful black animal took her eye particularly. He had a well-bred look about him, better than his fellows, and there was a certain challenge in the way he tossed his mane and stared boldly out between the railings, as though in contemplation of his chances of freedom from this dusty prison. Beside him as they wheeled once more, ran a grey – the only grey in the lot.

'That grey, Harry. He's a beauty, isn't he?'

The stockman shook his head in reply.

'Not like-um greyfella, missus.'

'Why ever not?' Rennie gazed after the lovely animal in surprise.

'Cattle not like-um that greyfella horse, missus,' ex-plained Harry with his usual patience. 'Allatime them ringers sing-um that mob at night, dem cattle t'ink him prop'ly ghost-horse, that-one, missus. They t'ink him might debil-debil. Him not good luck, eh?'

'You mean, the cattle are nervous of him just because he's *grey*?'

'You-ai, missus. Thatfella mob not sleep one-night, catchem debil-debil. If they bin fright-em, mebbe dey runout alonga dat scrub, plurry quick alonga 'nother-one country, allasame mebbe killem two, t'ree fella in thatone mob. More better not greyfella horse.' Again a shake of the sage, grizzled head.

Rennie looked from the unpopular grey back to the handsome black animal that had first taken her eye. Something in his challenging boldness kindled an answer-ing spark in her, spoke to that headstrong, wilful streak in her that had sometimes got her into trouble before.

Today wasn't the sort of day for trouble, though. Today the sun was shining and the world was at peace. Today she felt light-hearted, light-headed – elated – adventurous – free of all those responsibilities which had bowed her down for so long. Today she was answerable only to herself, and *for* herself!

And why not? What was to stop her? Nobody was around to see her. Nobody but Harry, and she could easily get around him. One only had to sound stern and authoritative, the way Chad did. One only had to command. Not *ask*, but *command*.

Harry's own horse was saddled a short distance off, the bridle slipped over one of the lower branches of a coolibah. On the fence a little way along from where Rennie was sitting lay another saddle, a light one that he used to get his pupils used to the feel of a strange and unfamiliar weight upon their backs. A couple of bridles were hanging on the gatepost.

Why not, indeed?

'That black horse there, Harry' – Rennie pointed him out – 'I want to ride him.'

'Not ride, missus. Nebber you ride. Catchem trouble that-way, eh?'

'Of *course* I can ride,' she retorted spiritedly. 'Just because you haven't seen me do it doesn't mean that I can't. I'll show you. Saddle him for me, will you, please, Harry?'

'Catchem trouble that-way,' he retorted, equally positively.

'But why? He's broken, isn't he? You just said that there are only two or three left that aren't. Anyway, I can see by the way he looks at me that he's just begging to get out of there. It's almost as if he's *asking* me to ride him, just to set him free.'

Harry loosed the rope on the colt, and eased it gently over the animal's trembling head, watched the young thing run off to the furthest corner of the yard. Then he came over to Rennie, put one booted foot on the lowest rail, and gazed up at her earnestly.

'Him broken all right, missus, but him proper crankyfella, that-one. Mebbe frightem allasame him killem you, eh.'

'Of course he won't hurt me, Harry! I tell you, I'm a good rider. I've been riding for years, over in England. In – in 'nother-one country, proper *long*-way,' she emphasized, resorting to Harry's own pidgin.

'S'pose him badfella, mightbe him killem you.' The dark features remained stubbornly set. Adamant.

There was only one thing to do.

'Saddle him up this minute, Harry, please. Otherwise I tell Bossfella, eh?'

The dark, grizzled head jerked up at that.

'Boss tellum you ride that-one, missus? *Chad* tellum you ride?'

It was immediately evident that Rennie had struck the right note. What Chad said was apparently not to be questioned.

'Would I be asking you to do it if he *hadn't* said it?' she countered, and succeeded in bringing such a note of injury and exasperation to her voice that Harry turned forthwith to take one of the bridles from the gatepost.

He mumbled as he went about catching and saddling the handsome black horse, who, now that freedom from that small yard had become a distinct possibility, had surprisingly turned difficult and reluctant – downright recalcitrant, in fact.

'Me not savvy which-way Chad tellum you prop'ly silly t'ing like that,' Harry grumbled, as he led the animal to the outer yard and returned the colt to the mob. 'Might him debil-debil, that Chad! Might Chad *sick-fella*!' He tapped his head significantly.

Rennie ignored those sotto voce remarks. Her blood was singing in her veins, whipping colour into her cheeks and bringing a sparkle of excitement to her sherry-gold eyes. She jumped down from her perch with the grace and agility of a young gazelle, and came over to her intended mount.

'You hold him while I get on, Harry. Then you can open the gate.'

'More better you ridem *here*, missus.' The stockman

attempted a final, half-hearted stand which Rennie ignored.

She grasped the reins, and in one swift leap was in the saddle, her feet seeking and finding the stirrups unerringly.

'Now open the gate,' she commanded – and Harry obeyed.

The black horse sidled through cautiously, stepping delicately in a sideways walk, neck arched, eye rolling. Rennie was aware that her mount was trembling from head to foot, barely schooled as he was and therefore apprehensive of the weight he carried, half-fearful of this sudden contact with that strange bi-ped, the human being. Although she was not holding him back, he appeared to be voluntarily curbing his enormous power of movement as if he were half afraid of it too.

Or that was what Rennie thought!

She dug her heel encouragingly into the black satin flank and was rewarded by immediate action. It was hardly the civilized action she had anticipated, though!

The next second found her fingers curling tighter on the reins, her body sloping backwards in an unconsciously appropriate reflex action as the proud black head plunged downward and the hind legs lashed out viciously.

It was the beginning of a battle of wills between horse and rider, and Rennie felt exhilaration sweep through her at the feel of those savage movements beneath her, exulted in the knowledge that her skill was being put to the test and would not be found wanting, that although the battle promised to be long and arduous, she possessed the balance and staying-power and experience to emerge the victor.

The black horse did not know it. Even if he had, he probably wouldn't have admitted it! He reared and rooted, bucked and twisted, and in between those frenzied gyrations, he made short, hysterical dashes over the soft, dusty ground between the yards and the buildings. The glint of the steel of machinery, the reflections of light upon glass windows, the mysterious, terror-ridden shadows of those unfamiliar human habitations drove him to fresh energies of despair.

Rennie was beginning to tire. Her muscles ached, and perspiration almost blinded her as her free hand sought and found the monkey-grip on the pommel, clung gratefully as they plunged together out into the open spaces once more, leaving those sheds behind.

The great black horse was beginning to tire too. Rennie sensed it, and drove her heels in hard. And then they were off – away in the maddest gallop of her whole life. Away from the homestead, away from the yards, away through a whistling kaleidoscopic tunnel of speed. The wind sang in her ears, the hoofbeats thudded, thundered. One falter, and they would surely go down!

She held her breath at the thought, then released it as she realized that she had won. She couldn't be dislodged now. She could ride like this for ever, over this wide brown plain, at this crazy pace. She would let the horse go on, because she was the victor now, for certain. In control. She could stop this very minute if she chose, but she would not do that. She would let her mount acquit himself first, gallop out the last feelings of rancour that might remain to him in defeat before she took him back to the yards.

And then she sensed a change in the atmosphere, in the drum-beats of those galloping hooves. They had suddenly become muddled and confused, ringing and pounding one upon another until there seemed to be thousands of them, echoing back in a giant tattoo of sound.

The black horse stretched his neck. He was flat out now. What an animal, to sustain this incredible speed! Rennie exulted wildly, and at almost the same moment it came to her that all of those echoing hoof-beats could not possibly be his alone.

They weren't!

Murtie was coming up fast on the near flank on a big bay gelding whose sides were flecked with foam. He was almost level with her now.

And now he *was* level.

He was coming in close, beyond her horse's neck, forcing him over, 'bending' him as he might bend the wayward leader of a mob of steers, turning him out of his mad gallop, turning him right into the path of Chad's speedy quarter-horse stallion, coming up on the other side, gauging its pace, biding its time with the innate intelligence of its breed for the moment when its grim-faced rider would lean out of the saddle and force that other, undisciplined animal to a standstill.

It dawned upon Rennie that both Murtie and Chad must think her own horse was out of control. She opened her mouth to call out, put pressure on the rein, but her words of reassurance were never uttered, for the big black rogue-horse took his own way out of the mad pursuit, reared up between the other two, and turned neatly to face the opposite direction and Rennie, caught completely unawares, slithered unceremoniously to the ground in a flurry of dust and flailing hooves.

Instinctively she lay face-down where she had fallen, putting her arms protectively over her head in a defensive gesture, remained there, inert, waiting for the thrashing movements that were going on about her to cease.

Then she felt strong hands sliding themselves beneath her body, and she was turned abruptly to face the sky. She screwed up her eyes against the glare of that bright, harsh light, and gazed apprehensively into Chad's grimly furious countenance. His features were whipped into unfamiliar lines, contorted with anger – or was it sheer exasperation?

'Renata?'

Those blazing eyes seared her, just as his tongue flailed her with that single, ground-out utterance.

Rennie found herself cringing before that glittering, green anger – and then, with returning spirit, she put her hands against his broad khaki shirt-front and tried to push him away.

'You spoilt it all!' she accused quiveringly, still fighting to regain her breath, because she had hit the ground with the sort of thump that leaves one temporarily speechless. 'You – if you hadn't—'

'Lie still, will you, please, till I make sure you haven't broken anything,' he interrupted coldly, tersely, un-

115

pleasantly – and Rennie was forced to submit to the touch of his searching brown hands as they ran expertly over her limbs.

Satisfied, Chad helped her none too gently to a sitting position, clapped his broad-brimmed hat back on his head, and stood up, squinting down at her.

'If I hadn't what?' he asked gratingly, and Rennie could see that he was still very angry. 'If I hadn't *what*?' He removed his hat again, and wiped the sweat from his brow with a curiously repressed impatience. 'You aren't fit to be left alone, I reckon! You aren't to be *trusted*! You might have broken your neck, at the very least! You could have *killed* yourself!' The deep voice thickened unrecognizably. 'Dammit all, don't look at me like that, either, or so help me, I'll spank you!'

Rennie dropped her injured gaze hastily. It was hard to appear anything *but* injured, sitting here in the dust right next to those long, khaki-clad legs in the elastic-sided boots, with Murtie grinning amusedly from a point somewhere behind Chad's shoulder, and well beyond the range of his employer's vision. She was at a disadvantage down here on the ground, in a heap in the dust at his feet. Undignified.

Rennie scrambled to her feet, swayed unexpectedly.

With one swift step, Chad was beside her again, and this time he did not let her go until he had half-carried her to a seat under a nearby shade-tree, where he deposited her hardly more gently and said,

'Get the water-bag, Murtie, will you? I reckon she could do with a drop.'

Rennie raised a pale, dusty face to find Chad's own uncomfortably near. His eyes were hard, and a tiny muscle flickered almost imperceptibly somewhere near his jaw-line.

'All right,' he said quietly, as Murtie ambled off to where he had tethered the horses, 'so you're one hell of a good rider and now we *all* know. Why couldn't you have said so before?'

He appeared to Rennie to be unreasonably annoyed over the whole thing. There was an almost dangerous quality about his self-control right now. The realization that she might say the wrong thing and unwittingly tip the balance was enough to render her silent and unresponsive.

'You've had ample opportunity to come out with it, Renata. All those times you've seen me coaching Magda, for instance. Oh, yes, I've been aware that you were watching!'

He got up from his squatting position at her side, thrust his hands into the pockets of his faded moleskins and paced restlessly to and fro in front of where she was sitting.

'Am I so unapproachable?' he flung at her stormily, after some moments. 'Or have I got the wrong angle on the whole thing? Perhaps everyone else *does* know that you ride a horse? Perhaps you've told *everyone*? Perhaps you've just waited till I'm away from the homestead, is that it? Maybe they all know – everyone but Chad Sandasen, is that it? The ogre uncle, the merciless guardian, is that how you see me, Renata?'

Rennie continued to gaze at him. For some reason, she was oddly disturbed by Chad's angry accusation. Tears stung her eyes, but she blinked them back as he went on—

'And what possessed you to demonstrate your skill on that rogue animal, anyway? He's dangerous, you must have realized that? The sort that always wants the last word. He's defied all Harry's and my own efforts to render him reliable. Where'd you get him, come to that? Come on, you'd better spill the beans. I have a right to know.'

She kicked at the dust, thankful to see Murtie returning with the waterbag. A third horseman was approaching, too – an angular black figure with a battered hat clamped on grizzled curls, and a pipe jutting out from his profiled mouth. Harry.

'Drink that, and then we're going home,' Chad told her brusquely. 'And I'll find out even if you don't tell me, I warn you. I'm not the Boss around here for nothing. *Somebody*'s hide is going to get scorched for allowing you to risk your neck on that brute!'

Rennie swallowed, decided she'd better get it over and done with.

'It was Harry,' she confessed awkwardly, 'but—'

'*Harry?*' Chad swung away from her to the newcomer, whose wide grin disappeared on the instant as he was asked crisply, 'What-name you let missus ride that cheeky-fella horse?'

'He didn't let me. I *made* him.' Rennie had got up again. Even standing, she was still dwarfed by Chad.

'Made him? How?' He turned again to the bewildered Harry. 'Which-way she make you?' he demanded.

Harry ignored the question. He was now grinning widely. It was a grin of singular charm, expansive, amused, appeasing. 'Py crikey, Boss! That youngfella missus putem plenty goodfella show, eh!' he enthused. 'When she tellem Harry Boss say she ride that-one cheeky horse, this fella bin t'ink might-be Boss bin sick belonga head.' He tapped his woolly pate suggestively. 'Now Harry savvy more better. She plenty good, eh, Boss?'

'Plenty good, Harry,' agreed Chad repressively. 'Now you catchem thatfella and yard him, understand? And, 'nother-one time, you not let youngfella missus ride cheeky horse, no matter *what* she tellum you. Savvy?'

Harry's liquid black eyes sharpened, his grin fading.

'You-ai, Boss.' He hesitated. 'Might that-one gammon me, Boss?' he asked uncertainly.

Chad's brow rose ironically as his eyes met Rennie's.

'Sure-thing she gammon you, Harry. Gammon alla-bout. That means "*everyone*",' he told Rennie in a silky aside. ' 'Nother-one time, you not listen to youngfella missus. Behind I tell you now, you only listen to *this* fella, eh, Harry?' He tapped his own broad chest. ' 'Nother-one time might her killem, see.'

'You-ai, Chad,' agreed the stockman readily, and then the irresistible grin broke once more. 'Allasame, young-fella missus she gammon that crankyfella black horse, *too*, eh, Boss? She prop'ly goodfella rider, that-one, mine t'inkit!'

Harry shook his head reflectively, slid a fleeting look of unmistakable admiration in Rennie's direction, and jogged

118

away in pursuit of his quarry.

'Mine t'inkit, too, Renata!' Murtie chuckled. 'You most certainly taught that black brute a lesson I reckon he never thought to get. He had it coming to him. And I really believe you had him in hand all the time.'

'Of course I did, Murtie. I was just letting him get the steam off, that was all. If you two hadn't come up like a pair of mad things, I'd have slackened him off when he tired. As it was, I still don't quite know what happened,' she admitted, giving the old man an answering smile, albeit a somewhat pallid one.

Chad's mouth twisted grudgingly.

'He only did what he's been taught to do. He swung on a sixpence, Renata. That is another way of saying that he turned right around almost in his own length, like every good stock-horse should be able to do, by the time Harry and I have finished with him! You must unwittingly have given him the signal.'

She looked mystified.

'I don't think I did. I – I don't think I did *anything*.'

'Then he did it himself,' Chad told her, and for the first time amusement chased the sternness from his expression. 'He's highly intelligent, that horse, but inclined to be wilful and disobedient – like someone else I could name right now,' he added, his mouth suddenly tightening again.

'You've gotter admit that Harry's right, though, eh, Chad?' insisted Murtie. 'You're some rider, Renata, you most certainly are! *Dead* sweet! It was just that turn that got you, that's all, and yer can't be blamed fer *that*, bein' a city rider.' The old man smiled at her kindly. 'It's like the poet said – Lawson, it was, you'll recall, Chad?—

"You may talk about your ridin' in the city, bold an'
    free,
Talk o' ridin' in the city, Texas Jack, but where'd
    you be
When the stock-horse snorts an' bundles all 'is quar-
    ters in a hump,
An' the saddle climbs a sapling, an' the horseshoes
    split a stump?"'

Chad's features relented at last.

'O.K., Murtie, you win,' he told the older man pleasantly – but there was a tiredness in his voice that Rennie had never detected before, a tiredness that was *more* than just his usual deep drawl. 'Now, let's get back to work. See that Harry gets that horse yarded again, will you, Murt? Come, Renata, I'm taking you home.'

'Home?' Barrindilloo, home? Well, she supposed it was that to Chad Sandasen, even if not to herself.

'Go on, up you go.' Chad held his stallion and placed a hand beneath her elbow.

Rennie opened her mouth to protest, caught the steely glint in his eye, the flicker of that tiny muscle as his jaw firmed, and decided not to argue. She fumbled her way into the saddle, stiff now, as her muscles protested at her recent fall, and Chad Sandasen swung up behind her and put his arm about her. As he urged his horse forward, he drew her back against him, clasping her body to him so that she could feel the steady beating of his heart through the cloth of the khaki bush-shirt that he wore. Or was it her own heart's beating, after all? It could be, for it was thudding uncomfortably quickly. Her own pulse-beat drummed in her ears, because she couldn't help her awareness of Chad Sandasen's arm about her, holding her to him. His bare forearm was right there whenever she dropped her eyes – sunburnt, muscular, fuzzed over thickly with bleached hairs that glinted against the brownness in the sun. His other hand held the reins loosely.

Rennie raised her eyes again, but somehow that brought the back of her head too near to his. She was conscious of his chin just behind her crown, could feel the warmth of his breathing close to her ear, could smell the mingled aroma of shaving lotion and dust and leather and tobacco that she had come to associate with Chad.

She dropped her head once more, and there was that arm again, steady and firm about her. It held her in a careful, impersonal sort of way. Rennie gazed at the rippling muscle, the strong wrist, the brown competent fingers – wondered what it would be like to be held by that arm in a way that *wasn't* careful, *wasn't* impersonal. Chad's hand was broad-backed, masculine, an 'outdoor' sort of hand. Yet it was also sensitive, incapable of clumsiness. Rennie had observed those same square-tipped fingers performing many tasks over the past weeks, and it occurred to her now that whatever they did, they possessed a sureness, an artistry, all their own, whether they were splicing a rope or plaiting a stockwhip or fixing a brand or a stencil, or simply rumpling Magda's hair or stroking his tanned, clean-shaven chin in that reflective manner in which he sometimes did when he was looking at Rennie herself in that uncomfortably penetrating way.

One good thing, sitting as she was now Rennie did not have to meet Chad's eyes. There was something for which to be thankful, because if he had been able to look into her face, he would surely have seen the delicate flush of colour creeping up amongst the dust and pallor at the trend her thoughts had taken.

The burnt plain stretched before them, mulga-dotted, shimmering in its own private lake of heat-reflections. High in the sky, a sparrow-hawk wheeled and floated, a drifting speck up there in the blue. Save for that distant, winging bird there were only herself and Chad and this horse in the whole wide world just now.

Only herself and Chad.

She cast a quick glance behind her, to his sternly set face.

Chad, at his most unreadable and enigmatic. His hat was pulled right down. Its brim was almost level with his jutting, sun-bleached brows, and his glittery eyes were narrowed as they so often were, looking right over the top of her head into the distance. They were green, unfathomable, slitted against the glare in that crinkled, wrinkled way which she had also come to associate with Chad. His mouth was set in a grim, straight line that made him seem at once remote, yet forbidding. Only the deep groove near its left-hand corner reminded her that that mouth could curve, with a sort of fascinating tenderness, into one of those rare curly smiles.

It wasn't smiling now, though. It was as grave, as remote, as the rest of him.

The little sparrow-hawk had gone. It had banked into the sun and glided right out of sight. A couple of crows had replaced it up there, flying lower on a ragged, indeterminate course, without the eagle grace of their predecessor, sky-high in the blueness. They emitted harsh, raucous cries that were like sad, slow laughs, as if they were deriding Rennie for her thoughts.

Har! Har! Har!

'I hate those horrid black birds,' she decided under her breath, 'and they're everywhere out here. Always waiting, watching. Probably just biding their time for some less fortunate creature to weaken and die. They're like this whole landscape – remorseless in a horrible, *patient* sort of way. Their cries are like warnings, doom-calls to the faltering.'

Rennie had seen the way those crows could descend to pick and pull at some unlucky carcase almost before oblivion had come to it. She knew that all forms of life must eat to survive, but there was something indecent about the haste with which they dropped down to their carrion meal, guided from miles of distance by an instinctive knowledge of death – or, worse, mere helplessness.

She shuddered, felt the immediate, reassuring tightening of Chad's arm pulling her closer, although he did not speak. The pine and tobacco aroma mingled with the dust thrown up by the stallion's cantering hooves.

The crows were circling above a wilga tree, and now they settled in its topmost branches and jeered. They looked like ragged pieces of torn black cloth fluttering amongst the boughs. She was glad that they followed no further, even though it meant that there were now just herself and Chad and the horse again. Rennie could do without those crows!

It seemed unbelievable that that black rogue-horse had brought her so far in his maddened gallop. Rennie had been expecting to see the homestead buildings materializing on the horizon for the last mile or so. When they did, she could scarcely conceal a sigh of pure relief.

She stiffened away from Chad, leaning forward over the stallion's withers, and made a pretence of patting the sweat-foamed neck. It was wet beneath her fingers.

The animal did not stop at the saddling-yard, but was urged on by its rider until it came to a halt at the gate in the white paling fence that surrounded the house.

There, Chad swung down, passed the reins through the stirrup, looked up at Rennie, and held out his arms to take her as she dismounted.

As he stood there, booted and spurred, with his wide felt hat tipped back on his head as he looked up, she noted with some surprise that he was paler than usual. Those strange, eucalyptus-green eyes were inscrutable, but there was a sober, purposeful, *waiting* quality in him that caused a sudden flutter of pure panic in Rennie just then.

When one allows oneself to be overwhelmed by panic, one is apt to do something stupid, and afterwards she was forced to admit that her next, confused action was both ill-considered and foolish, and with a result far more disastrous and unexpected than she could ever have anticipated.

Rennie had scarcely scrambled awkwardly down upon the other side of the horse – the *wrong* side – than she felt a vice-like grip on her elbow, and she was turned violently and precipitately, without volition, right into Chad Sandasen's arms.

If she had thought herself close to him up there in the saddle, it was nothing to what she was now. His arms were like steel bands about her, forcing her against him, so that she could feel the hardness of his thigh muscles against her own through the thin denim cloth of her once-smart, dusty jeans. The buckle of his low-slung kangaroo-hide belt dug sharply into her soft flesh through her shirt, and her face was muffled into his khaki-clad chest in a way that made breathing difficult.

Rennie managed to turn her head sideways, took a grateful gulp of air, her mind lurching so crazily that it was impossible to think.

Chad's fingers forced her chin up so that she had to look at him.

'You've been avoiding me, Renata,' he accused, and even his voice seemed strange and thick and unfamiliar to her reeling senses. 'Why?'

He shook her almost savagely, and Rennie could only blink.

What was this? A dream? A nightmare? Was it really happening?

It *was*!

And it went right on happening, too!

Rennie knew, instinctively, a split second before he did it, just what Chad meant to do. She could read his purpose, right there in his eyes. They were like cold silver streams, drowning her in their icy depths, narrowed and calculating. When his lips came down on hers, they, too, were cool. Cool and firm and forceful. Brutal. Ruthless.

Rennie struggled, knew the futility of it. There was no escape from those cool, firm, seeking lips.

There was no passion in Chad Sandasen's kiss – only anger, a deadly self-assurance and a certain experienced thoroughness. When he finally put her away from him, Rennie stood quivering, her vision blurred, instinctively covering her bruised lips with the back of a hand that shook visibly.

The man whose eyes sought hers so boldly was well aware of that shaking hand, Rennie knew, and despised herself for the trembling that she was unable to control. Speechlessly she watched him raise his hat and re-settle it at a lower angle over his brow with a gesture that almost mocked.

'If there has to be a *reason* for keeping out of my way, Renata, you've got one now,' Chad told her smoothly.

And then he turned away, flung the reins over his horse's head, swung up into the saddle again and rode off without a backward glance, leaving Rennie standing there near the small white gate in the paling fence with her hand still pressed to her lips, gazing dully after him.

CHAPTER SEVEN

ASH RYARTON was in a teasing mood next morning.

'You've made headlines on the galah today, Rennie,' he joked.

'I?' She was startled.

'Weren't you listening in? You should have been,' Ash rebuked her somewhat whimsically. 'The whole world knows we've a crack rider here on Barrindilloo now, according to Elspeth.'

'Oh!' Rennie was embarrassed – actually relieved, too, that it was only her riding that was the apparent subject of that gossipy interchange on the open transceiver session this morning. Her cheeks were scarlet with the memory that obsessed her own thoughts today – that of Chad Sandasen's punishing kiss!

'H-how could they possibly know?' she collected herself sufficiently to ask Ash, bringing her mind to what he was saying with an effort.

He leaned on the corner of his desk and shrugged.

'That's the biggest unsolved mystery that ever was, Rennie, I guess – how these little titbits get abroad without even the aid of the mulga wire! They've got it, anyway, the whole darn story. Elspeth says the listeners were delighted at the sheer improbability of it all – the young English model girl at Barrindilloo who put on a rodeo all on her own.' He chuckled. 'They're all delighted, except, probably, for one person, and that's Leith. She likes to be the best girl rider we've got in these parts. She won't care to have her position threatened by an outsider – and a Pommy one at that! Maybe that's why Chad's gone off this morning – to simmer her down a bit. He's an artful cove when it comes to soothing sheilas' ruffled feathers!'

'Gone off?' Rennie blinked, scarlet again. 'Has he gone *away*?'

Ash nodded.

'In his plane, this morning. With his best city duds on, too. Looked as if he could be planning a week-end on the tiles in one of the capitals, if you ask me. Probably he'll call for Leith and take her with him.'

Rennie thought that over.

A vision of Leith's pretty red head beside Chad's own swarthy one in that lovely silver aeroplane had no particular appeal this morning. She supposed she was feeling sour with the whole world, that was why! She had slept only fitfully, and when the kookaburras started laughing – in the dawn of a new day, down at the creek, they had seemed to be deriding her, just as those nasty black crows had done yesterday.

Hoo-hoo – haha! Hoo-hoo – haha! they had mocked, and Rennie had turned her head into her pillow, trying to shut out the sound.

'Don't you ever go, too, Ash – when he goes off like that?' She determinedly controlled her thoughts again. 'Don't you ever *want* to go, just for the ride?'

The book-keeper grimaced.

'I've told you how it is with me, Rennie. I'd go actually, sometimes – just for the ride, as you say. But permanently, never. I reckon this is my home. I feel sort of odd down there in the Big Smoke now. I'm not as young as I used to be, you know. My days of doing the town all night, like Chad does, are past! I suppose I'll end my days here, now that I'm back.'

Murtie unwittingly echoed Ash's pronouncement later that very morning.

'So Chad's off on the skite, is 'e?' he asked interestedly. 'I *thought* somethin' was bitin' him earlier this mornin', when he came clatterin' down ter the camp around piccaninny daylight. 'E must've got the itch overnight!' He sighed. 'I wouldn't of minded stowin' away fer a jaunt meself, on'y three's a crowd, and it's a fair bet he'll be takin' Leith Mindon with 'im, if you arst me.'

Rennie *hadn't* asked him. She *certainly* hadn't! Why on earth did everyone have to talk about Leith Mindon this morning – Leith and Chad? First Ash, and now Murtie.

'What would you do if you went with Chad, Murtie? If you stowed away?'

Murtie bared his tobacco-stained teeth in a sheepish grin.

'Make a beeline fer the nearest pub, prob'ly, an' have a bit of a bender,' he confessed amiably, 'just like a drover's bullock'll make fer that water-hole after a dry stage. I like it fer a while, see, Renata. But the city life fer keeps'd be enough ter give me white ants in the billy, s'truth, it would!' Murtie tapped his grey head comically.

'Don't you ever feel you've *missed* anything, Murtie, living away out here?' she asked curiously, looking away to those far, endless, monotonous horizons. 'I mean, all this space and just a handful of people, and knowing there are other exciting places, crammed with sights and sounds and all the wonderful man-made advances that you can't possibly experience out here?'

'Huh!' Murtie unstuck his cigarette from between his lips and waved it in front of his face disparagingly. 'Sometimes, when man *advances*, God *retreats*,' he told her cuttingly. 'You earmark that, young Renata, an' think it over.'

'Then you don't have any regrets?'

'Regrets? Fer what?' the old man shook his head firmly. 'Reckon I'm too old ter start regrettin', Renata. I wouldn't know where ter begin, an' where ter leave off. No, I reckon I'm like the poet said –

> "For good undone and gifts misspent and resolutions
>   vain,
> 'Tis somewhat late ter trouble. This I know –
> I should live the same life over, if I had ter live
>   again,
> And the chances are I go where most men go."

'That's *my* philosophy, as well, I reckon, Renata. She's a beaut philosophy, that – an' I'll probably go somewhere a good bit hotter than what it is here at Barrindilloo, too!'

He chuckled wickedly. Murtie, the incorrigible!

Rennie found herself grinning back understandingly before she sauntered back towards the homestead to help Elspeth start the lunch.

That evening, Chad's place at the head of the table was conspicuously empty and next day it was the same. But on Sunday, as dusk was falling, there was a droning noise in the sky as his Aztec banked over the homestead and settled on to the landing-strip.

Rennie felt her stomach muscles tighten in a curious way, and when she went to the veranda to peer out through the gauze, she found that she had consciously to unclench her fingers which were curled tightly into her palms.

It was something of a surprise to find that Chad had not returned alone.

As he came through the white gate and crossed the lawns to the front steps, Leith Mindon walked at his side. Chad carried a pigskin case as well as his own week-ender, and Rennie could only presume that it must belong to the pretty red-headed girl for whom he was even now opening the gauze-meshed door.

Leith smiled, stepped delicately in on to the veranda and Chad removed his broad-brimmed hat and fol-lowed.

' 'Evening, Renata.' Rennie didn't receive the same warm smile as Chad had done. Instead, the girl's manner was reserved, noticeably cooler than it had been that other time they had met.

She walked along the veranda to the guest-room, and Chad carried her case in that direction too. Leith knew her way about this house very well indeed. It was obvious that she had adopted a certain authority and pos-sessiveness when within its walls, almost as if she were already the mistress of Barrindilloo homestead, and not just the *intended* mistress!

At tea-time that same night, she took her place at the opposite end of the table to Chad himself. This secretly surprised Rennie, who had thought she would probably wish to sit beside him on his right-hand side, in the guest's place of honour. It seemed, however, that Leith preferred the role of hostess to that of visitor. She signalled to Mayra to place the huge silver teapot before her so that she could pour, and a short time afterwards it was she who rang for the water-jug to be replenished.

'I must show Nellie how to keep this silver from getting tarnished,' she remarked pleasantly to Ash at one point, peering critically at the embossed leaf-design on the jug. 'And I think she's leaving half the polish there, without rinsing it properly afterwards, too. Those lubras will get off with anything if they're allowed. They're apt to think a nice wide smiles makes up for all sorts of laxness and deficiencies.'

'It was I who cleaned the silver last,' Rennie admitted hastily, lest the innocent Nellie should be blamed for something for which, this time at least, she most certainly was not responsible. 'Perhaps I'm not very good at it,' she added humbly.

'Hardly your line, is it,' said Leith sweetly, 'so I suppose you can be forgiven. Lack of domesticity probably doesn't matter a hoot in the model girl's world, but I can assure you that a practical background is of great importance when running an isolated homestead such as this one, and especially when dealing with those lazy aboriginal girls. One must be able to do everything one expects one's underlings to do – and do it a great deal better than they, at that!' She popped a small square of buttered toast into her mouth, and when she had eaten it, went on to observe modestly, 'I've been fortunate to have been doing that sort of thing all my life, ever since I was quite small. Now it's second nature to me – no effort, although of course I love the outdoor life even more than the indoor one. I can understand you saying the Outback is so boring, though, Renata, and it's only to be expected, really.'

Rennie's brows rose in surprise. 'I?' She blinked. 'I don't remember saying any such thing!'

Leith's eyes rested on the other girl's slowly flushing face with some amusement.

'Oh, come now, of course you did! No need to be coy in front of Chad, just because we all know he's so wrapped up in his beloved Barrindilloo. No need to spare his feelings by pretending, even if we *were* having a girlish exchange of confidences at the time. He's not in the least offended, are you, darling?'

Now it was Chad's turn to look at Rennie. He did so with one of those penetrating and discomfiting glances, for whose brevity on this particular occasion Rennie was thankful.

'Not in the least,' she was politely assured, in a deep, uncompromising tone. 'It's quite understandable that you should feel that way, Renata. As Leith so truly says, it's only to be expected.'

But I don't! I didn't! Rennie wanted to protest – and to her own astonishment she realized that that was true. There was so much here that she *didn't* find boring, even though she might have thought she would. So much! There were all her friends, for instance – the comfortable Elspeth, the undemanding Ash, the irrepressible Murtie, those two laughing, dark-eyed lubras and the mischievous Harry Goola with his smelly, funny old pipe. There was the chuckling kookaburra and the shrilling cockatoo, the wind that came in warm gusts off the plain and sighed so pensively in the coolibahs, the yapping of the dogs and the yabbering of the piccaninnies, the possum that swung so cheekily from his tail and peered inquisitively into the light of Magda's torch when its beam discovered him, the scuttling black water-hens down at the pool and the cock that crowed a mournful salute as Chad's heavy steps sounded along the veranda in the first hushed light before the sun rose each day.

She swallowed. *Why* had Leith attributed such an impossible remark to her? she wondered, distressed. *When* had this 'girlish exchange' taken place? Rennie could not remember any such occasion, try as she might. Why, the fact was that she had seen too little of Leith for there even to have been an opportunity for such a discussion!

'It was kind of you to clean the silver, Renata.' Chad's voice spoke quite gently beside her. His eyes were suddenly quizzical and kind as if he sensed her distress, though of course he could not possibly guess at the reason.

'Especially as you aren't accustomed to doing such things.'

'Don't mention it,' Rennie returned shortly. She felt angry, ruffled. Angry with *both* of them. She wished – oh, how she wished – that Leith Mindon had not come back tonight to stay! Of how long she was intending to remain neither she nor Chad had so far given any indication. As for Leith herself, she gave the impression that she was permanently installed, or would like to be!

Things weren't the same as they had been at all, now that she was here. The air prickled with unspoken comments, the silences were somehow fraught and tense, and nobody seemed to be behaving normally any more. Magda turned suddenly fractious. Ash became withdrawn and cautious, Elspeth was no more than respectfully civil, and Nellie and Mayra flitted around the table like a couple of nervous and gaudy butterflies in their bright cotton overalls, their thin hands trembling as they grabbed at the dishes with unfamiliar haste.

After the meal, Leith rose from her chair and went away to the veranda with Chad, having first asked Mayra to bring drinks there.

'*Two* glasses,' she had requested, 'some sliced lemon. And *please* be sure that the water is iced.'

It wasn't until she was getting ready for bed that she saw Leith again that evening. Rennie was seated at her dressing-table in her soft voile peignoir, of a vivid peacock-blue which Rennie particularly liked, and which somehow made her pale blonde hair seem even lighter than usual, like liquid gold spilling over her shoulders. Rennie turned when she heard a step outside and when the door opened, saw that it was Leith who entered.

'Hullo.' Leith herself was still dressed. 'I'm just off to bed, too. Thought I'd just look in to say good night.'

She sank down in the only armchair in the room and eyed Rennie with interest as she began to cleanse her face with the meticulous thoroughness of her profession. As their gazes met in the reflected glass, she smiled and remarked generously,

'What marvellous hair you have, Renata! I suppose

that's how you got to be a model in the first place.'

Rennie smiled back. Leith was undoubtedly in a more friendly mood.

'That, and a lot of hard work as well. It isn't all fun, you know. There's a tremendous amount of self-discipline attached to it if you want to be successful – and a good proportion of luck as well,' she added honestly.

'And you were lucky?'

Rennie thought about that. She thought of those tiresome, endless sessions of posing, changing, posing; of the early mornings, the late nights; the flashing bulbs; the clipped instructions, the terse commands, the applause if all went well. But it hadn't all been like that, of course. There'd been those trips to the sun, away from England's capricious climate, to faraway, exotic places, to r leve the tedium and vary the pace. It all seemed a world away, now. Unreal, a rather improbable, dream.

'Yes, I believe I was lucky,' she returned thoughtfully, reaching for a tissue in the box beside her. 'I got all the breaks that were going. I was lucky.'

Here at Barrindilloo there was sun, too. Plenty of it. All the sun one could possibly want. Sun and peace and time to think. In a way, there was an exotic quality about this place, too. In its individuality it was every bit as strange and exciting as the Bahamas and Bermuda and Majorca and Corfu – even as exciting, probably, as Fez would have turned out to be! Rennie had a feeling that there possibly wasn't another place in the whole world quite like Barrindilloo. It was unique, just as every great lonely cattle station was of itself unique – each carrying an identity, a character, all its own.

'You miss it?'

Rennie thought some more.

'It's difficult to give a straight answer to that,' she said hesitantly. 'In ways, I do.'

'But you'll be going back to it very soon now, won't you? When are you actually planning to leave?'

'*Leave?*' Somehow, Rennie was startled. With Leith's last question came the astonishing realization that it was several days since the thought of leaving Barrindilloo had even entered her mind. Days. Nearly a week, in fact.

'Yes, *leave*.' Leith had straightened up in a business-like way. Her former idle, friendly manner had again disappeared. 'I seem to remember that you were to come in order to see Magda safely installed and settled. Well, she *is*, isn't she? She appears perfectly at home here, so far as I can observe – and that is one of the particular reasons for my visit just now, to ascertain just how she has settled down. It's more than obvious that she's happy. Her lessons seem to be progressing, she works the set herself for the School session each morning, joins in the chatter, rides her pony. She's attached to Elspeth and Ash, and one would almost say that Chad is her *idol*. I believe she actually prefers him to you,' finished Leith with surprising and calculated cruelty.

Rennie felt the chill shock of surprise at the other girl's sudden volte-face. It feathered over her in an unpleasant, shivering wave. In the mirror she could see herself paling visibly, so that her complexion was as white as the cream she had daubed in tiny dots upon her cheeks. Her eyes seemed enormous, hollow, bewildered.

'What are you trying to say?' she managed to ask quietly, trying to mask the apprehension in her question. 'You didn't come here just to wish me good night, I think, Leith, after all – did you?'

The other looked faintly uncomfortable, but determined.

'You're quite right, Renata, I didn't. I came because *one* of us had to, and Chad—' She shrugged meaningly, continued, '*One* of us had to point out to you that you can't go on trespassing on his hospitality for ever. After all, a bargain is a bargain. He has kept his side of it, so don't you think, now that the object of your mission has been accomplished, that the time has come for you to retire gracefully?'

The silence in the room was oppressive. It seemed to settle over Rennie in a sort of smothering cloud, so that she felt herself fighting for breath.

Oh, this was awful! Ghastly! Unbelievable! That they

should have to *ask* her to leave! That Chad should find her presence here at his homestead so – so intolerable that he found it necessary to enlist Leith's help in getting rid of her!

Rennie recalled that brutal kiss with a shiver. It lay between them now, an embarrassment to him, obviously. He wanted her out of his way now, just as quickly as possible, and in truth, there was no reason why she should have stayed even as long as she already had. It was just that she had suddenly found that the days were rushing by without her even noticing how fast they sped. Of *course* she was longing to go! Of *course* she was wanting to see Magda settled, to get back to Keith! Hadn't her heart been singing over that very prospect when she had wandered down to the yards the other day? And it was since *that* day – that kiss! – that Chad had suddenly found her very *being* here quite insupportable! What a blow to one's pride, to be asked to leave in this manner, when one had been intending to go quite soon in any case! Already her welcome here had been clearly outstayed – ever since the moment when Chad's firm, cool lips had come down upon hers in that calculatedly chastising manner. Since that very moment, she'd been outstaying her welcome with every minute that she spent here, and now they'd found it necessary to *ask*. They'd discussed it between them, discussed *her*!

Rennie's cheeks were suffused with hot colour. She put her hands up to her face, and her palms felt hot and moist too.

'I – of course I shall go,' she said in a strangled voice. 'I – I'll leave tomorrow.'

There was a perceptible change in Leith's expression, a quickly controlled surprise at Rennie's precipitate offer of co-operation. Such a reaction had been clearly unexpected.

'No, not tomorrow,' she replied firmly – and you'd have said there was almost actual *alarm* behind that firmness. 'Let's keep it civilized, shall we? I mean, you don't want to embarrass Chad by just rushing off suddenly, do you? And what would Magda think? And the rest of the people here, if you just dropped everything and left without any prior announcement?' She smiled more kindly as she continued appeasingly, 'No, Renata, I didn't mean *that*, and I'm sorry if my talking to you like this has caused you any unnecessary distress. All I meant to point out was that the time has come when you should be thinking of a departure date, at least a tentative one. For Magda's sake. And ours. Chad's and mine. You'll need to wait till after the race meeting. After all, Chad put it off till now on account of you and Magda coming, so it would be a bit churlish not to be there for it. But once it's over you could just sort of say, "Well, I think it's time I was getting back to work," or something – quite casually, just as one normally would do – and then go. I think that would be the best and most tactful thing to do, don't you?'

'Y-yes, of course. Whatever you suggest,' muttered Rennie, still upset. 'I – I'm sorry if I'm in the way. I—'

'No, you aren't in the way, not in the *meantime*,' Leith stressed soothingly. 'It's just that Chad and I — well, Chad thinks I should start cultivating a deeper relationship with Magda as soon as possible, and I really can't start while *you're* here, can I? I'll do very much better once I have her to myself.'

'Yes, I can see that,' Rennie acknowledged fairly. She felt herself drooping with weariness, as exhausted as if she had run a ten-mile race. 'I'll do as you have said, Leith. And – I – I'm truly sorry you found it necessary to prod me on like this. I should have realized that it was time I handed over the reins, as I agreed with Chad that I would do in the first place, providing Magda was happy here.'

'Don't mention it.' Leith stood up, apparently satisfied. She spoke almost gaily. 'I knew you'd see it that way, Renata. Well, I really must go to bed now. Chad has promised to take me for an early morning ride tomorrow. Good night.'

'Good night, Leith.'

Rennie performed the rest of her toilet that night woodenly, gazing unseeingly at her reflected image, hardly aware of what she was doing. Then she crept between the sheets, and oddly enough, slept almost at once.

Even her mind seemed vacant, numb, so that her thoughts did not torment her, as they otherwise might have done. Her brain was a void, and there were no thoughts there at all, just a woolly sort of unreal feeling.

When the kookaburras started their dawn-time laughter to ensure that the world might enjoy another day, Rennie heard *two* lots of steps along the veranda this time – Chad's own familiar, measured ones, and a brisk, light tap-tap that Leith's daintier riding-boots made on the boards as they followed. Shortly after that came the sound of thudding hooves as their horses cantered off, away from the homestead buildings towards the open plain.

Two days later Leith left to return to her own home.

Mail-days at Barrindilloo always held a certain amount of excitement, but the one some days after Leith had left proved more rewarding than usual for Rennie, for it contained a letter for her from Keith.

An air of expectancy always hovered over the entire homestead when mail-day came around. You somehow knew, from the first waking moment in the morning, that this was going to be a day quite different from the others. The frogs trilled louder from the edge of the creek, and the kookaburras chuckled more jubilantly than usual to tell the inhabitants of their locality that something special was going to happen.

The men did not go out from the homestead on this particular day. Instead, others rode in. From early morning there was a steady stream of newcomers trickling over the plain towards the homestead, many of them people whom Rennie did not know. They sat about under the shade-trees down near the quarters, yarning with the station-hands and jackeroos, swopping tobacco and papers and improbable stories, until the moment arrived when they all stood up and came out from under the trees to tilt their hats and squint up into the sun as the drone of the mail-plane impinged upon their conversation, and the light reflected upon its tilting silver wings. On this day, too, both Chad and Ash were apt to retire immediately after breakfast to their respective offices, to deal with the last of their outgoing correspondence, while Elspeth busied herself in the kitchen preparing the pilot's favourite dishes, in exchange for the titbits of gossip she could expect to receive from him while he ate.

Rennie felt, firstly, an element of pure surprise as she recognised Keith's writing, and secondly, a sensation of genuine puzzlement. How had he known that she was here? How had he known where to find her?

Many times since her arrival at Barrindilloo she had stifled the impulse to write to him and let him know where she was, sorely tempted though she had been, for she felt bad about the way she and Magda had simply disappeared that morning without so much as a word. Rennie had at that stage been so convinced that she would have to return to Sydney, and eventually to England, with Magda, and retain her guardianship of the child, that Keith's unexpected re-entry into her life – so heaven-sent, so unbelievable! – had suddenly become a fresh complication. Chad Sandasen himself, the debonair, suave, sunburnt, outback tyrant, had been a severe shock to Rennie's innocent preconceptions of what lay in store for little Magda. So had this whole set-up at remote Barrindilloo, come to that! Far better to forget that tantalising pang of promise, that deliciously piquant emotion that Keith Stamford had re-awakened in her! Better, at least, to forget it until she could be sure that she would be free to go to him this time, on the terms he had previously laid down – terms which Rennie knew she just had to accept as being a part of Keith himself, because of the overwhelming nature of her love for him.

Just lately she had allowed herself to acknowledge with more than her former caution the validity of Chad's claims upon the child. All evidence pointed to the fact that Barrindilloo could provide a suitable upbringing for Magda – indeed, a far more promising one than she herself could ever expect to provide. It now appeared, too, that Chad Sandasen was about to remedy the only part of the arrangement which left anything to be desired by way of proxy parenthood, and that was his state of bachelordom. And who better to alter that status than the lovely Leith Mindon? Beautiful, accomplished, a native of the area by birth and inclination, she would make an excellent mistress of Barrindilloo homestead. As a wife for Chad – well –

Unaccountably, Rennie's mind veered away from that line of thought.

Her fingers shook with pure excitement as she slit the envelope and extracted the sheets which Keith had covered with his familiar curly writing.

'My darling, *naughty* Rennie' – he had written – 'how dared you disappear like that! And without even leaving a note or a message! It was too bad of you, and I went through agonies wondering why you did such a thing. I can only suppose it was to pay me back, in kind, for the time I walked out on you after our stupid quarrel. If revenge was your object, then you were certainly successful! Oh, my darling! – if only you knew what fresh tortures you put me through, and just when I thought we had found each other again. I can't tell you what overwhelming relief I felt when I got Sandasen's letter and learned where you were. I must say it's decent of him to have invited me up for the Barrindilloo race meeting. I've heard of it, of course, but had no idea he had any connection with it. I couldn't even remember the name of the company that fellow gave when he met you at Mascot, although I went back and asked at the information desk. I guess I was so delighted to see you again that I just didn't take it in! At the Eucalypt Grove they would only say that they weren't permitted to discuss clients, but that you'd left no forwarding address. From what Sandasen said, the brat has settled down well with him, so it looks as if that's our little obstacle out of the way at last. She never took to me, nor I to her, so things just wouldn't have panned out so long as she was tagging after you. But now – well, that's a different story! I've got loads of plans for us – strictly honourable ones, this time! – plans that I know you'll find as exciting as I do.

'Just think, in only a week I'll be seeing you again. The mere thought is a sweet torment, because each hour I'm away from you seems like a year, and a week is eternity. But I'll be there, my sweet. I've rearranged my flight ops.

138

so that leave coincides, and I understand there's a charter plane going up with all the Sydney lovelies aboard as well, which should be fun. But none so fair as you, my adored one! Till tomorrow week, then, think of me, my precious – as I shall be, constantly, of you. Keith.'

Rennie's eyes were glowing, her cheeks suffused with colour, as she replaced the letter in its envelope. Impulsively, she rose to her feet and, still with the letter in her hand, walked along the veranda and knocked at the door of Chad's office.

'Come in, please.'

He was seated, as she had guessed he would be, at his roll-topped desk, sorting through his own newly-received mail. As she entered, he got up out of his swivel-chair, his brows lifting in surprise.

'It's you, Renata! What brings you? Would you like to sit down?'

Today, simply because it was mail-day and he was staying in the vicinity of the homestead, Chad was wearing a white shirt whose sleeves were neatly rolled up, a multi-striped tie, and pale cord trousers instead of his customary khakis. Even in his shabbiest and most faded clothing he looked indisputably what he was – the Boss of Barrindilloo Station. Like this, he still retained that distinctive air of quiet authority about him, of course, but there was an added quality as well, that one of which Rennie had been so suffocatingly aware the very first time she had ever met him. It was an indefinable 'something' compounded of casual strength and careless elegance, of a sunburnt ruggedness and an easy, animal grace in the way he held his head and carried those broadly powerful shoulders. The whole effect was of a debonair and rather lazily handsome villain. The laziness, as she knew now, was deceptive, an illusion. With the swarthy tan and curiously glinting green eyes and almost menacingly authoritative manner, he could have been a pirate captain about to order her to walk the plank.

Instead, he ordered her, politely and impersonally, to be seated.

So much for her temerity in invading his private

sanctum like this, although she was sure his expression would have been more yielding and inviting if it had been Leith Mindon who had entered just now, instead of herself!

'And what can I do for you?'

'It's – just – er – this.' Rennie took the chair he had brought forward and tapped the envelope. 'It's from Keith.'

'Yes?' The green eyes were narrowed, attentive, unrevealing.

Rennie blushed. She wished now that she hadn't been so impulsive as to come here, after all.

'I – he tells me that you have invited him to the – er – race meeting. I was so surprised and p-pleased that I wanted to thank you, that's all,' she stammered uncomfortably. It sounded silly, somehow.

'Don't mention it.' His voice was dry. Cool.

'What I can't understand is why you did it?'

'Why I did *what*?'

'Why you invited Keith. *How* you invited him.'

A shrug of the wide shoulders. Chad searched his pockets for tobacco, papers, began to rub the tobacco carefully between his palms. He took his time before replying at all.

'It wasn't hard to contact him. There was only one Captain Stamford flying with that particular airline. The chances against there being two were understandably remote. As for *why*—' he raised his eyes and gave her a level, inscrutable look – 'he is a friend of yours, is he not, Renata?'

'Yes, but—'

'A *special* friend?' Chad was insistent. His eyes were oddly hard now, and again she was aware of his dominant personality, his masculine authority which almost dared her to negate that statement.

'Yes, a – a dear friend,' she admitted, half defiantly, unable to determine the trend of his thoughts.

'Exactly. A *dear* friend.' Chad appeared to be satisfied with the cigarette which he had finished. He licked the edge of the paper, stuck it down with a single deft stroke, and tapped the finished article on his thumb-nail. 'That was the precise reason for my inviting him, Renata, the fact that he's a special friend. People are apt to pair off a little bit these days at social functions, and the race meeting is no exception. I didn't want you to feel out of it.'

'Oh, I see.'

So that was the way! Rennie swallowed. She could see the sense of his reasoning, of course, so why should she feel this little niggle of dissatisfaction, as if, somehow, Chad had actually evaded answering her question. He *had* answered it, hadn't he, though? And what he had said *did* make sense. Indeed, she would even go so far as to say it had been extraordinarily thoughtful of him, to go to all that bother tracking down Keith, writing, everything, just so that she would not find herself alone. Naturally, he himself would be squiring Leith Mindon. She and Chad would be amongst those who'd be 'pairing off a little bit', as he had rather vaguely expressed it. There was nothing vague about Chad's *intentions*, though, even if that phrase – 'pairing off a little bit' – sounded that way! After all, Leith herself had made that perfectly plain, in a way that had not been vague at all. 'Chad and I,' she'd said, and, 'I came because *one* of us had to.'

Rennie put her hands to her burning cheeks as she recalled the other girl's meaningful, rather spiteful, words. They had been discussing her, Leith and Chad. They'd put their heads together, discussing their future, talking about Rennie and how they could get her *out* of that future as soon as possible, because she had been too stupidly blind to see just how little she was wanted around here now.

Rennie was almost sure that they had talked about *this*, too. Between them, they had decided to invite Keith up, not so much so that Rennie wouldn't feel out of it, as so that Rennie would not be *in the way*. It had been a combined decision – Leith's and Chad's.

That new realization somehow took a little of the gladness from the prospect of seeing Keith. It had managed to spoil things just the tiniest bit, although she was still looking forward madly to seeing him – of *course* she was!

'Something wrong?' Chad's deep voice broke into her thoughts. He was watching her quietly as he drew on his cigarette.

'What? Oh – er – no. I – I was just th-thinking.' Rennie dropped her hands from her scarlet face.

'Well, don't get *too* excited *too* early, will you?' advised Chad drawlingly. 'You've a whole week to go yet, Renata, before you'll be seeing him, I'm afraid.'

'Yes. Yes, I know.' Her thoughts were more confused than ever. She got up. 'I must go and help Elspeth,' she said abruptly, and without attempting to delay her, he too rose to his feet and gravely held open the door.

The week that followed passed more quickly than Rennie would have thought possible. In her sudden awareness that her time at Barrindilloo Station was soon coming to a close, it was as if the minutes had decided obligingly to speed their progress until the moment when Keith would be here. Even Chad himself appeared to be making an extra effort – a *personal* effort – to fill those hours for Rennie so that they would soon pass, and when he somewhat surprisingly invited her to accompany himself and Magda upon one of their frequent swimming expeditions, she accepted with a pleasure she did not try to conceal.

What fun to be included! She had so often seen those two walking off in the direction of the creek. Chad's long lean frame, khaki-clad. Magda's tiny, fair-haired figure bobbing along beside him, with her bathers and towel wrapped in a bundle under her arm. Rennie had wondered where they went, where they swam, and what they did. And now, almost on the eve of her departure from this place, she was about to find out. She had been *invited*!

Rennie hesitated over her bikini, replaced it in her drawer and put on a buttercup-yellow swimsuit. It was a demure, stretch-towelling affair that somehow accentuated her beautifully proportioned body and slender, tanned limbs just as successfully, but much more subtly, than the bikini would have done. Recalling Chad's sarcastic mouth, his biting reference to the bareness of her backless evening gown, she told herself that he could hardly find much fault with the modesty of this particular garment.

Apparently he liked what he saw. Rennie knew it, instinctively, by the kindling gleam in his narrowing green eyes as they appraised her coolly, although he said not a word. Instead, he pulled off his shirt and trousers to reveal plain black bathing trunks with a white side-stripe, and dived cleanly into the clear green pool in a graceful arc that left almost no splash as he disappeared beneath the water. He surfaced some yards away, shaking his wetly dark hair from his eyes like a terrier.

'Coming in?'

'Is it cold?'

'Come and see.'

It was an idyllic afternoon. After the swim they lay on towels in the hot sun, drying almost immediately. Presently Chad rolled over on to his back, reached for his hat, and put it over his face.

'I believe you really enjoyed that, Renata.' The brim of the hat muffled his voice.

'Yes, I did.' Her own voice was eager – so eager that Chad pushed back the hat and looked at her.

'I think you enjoy quite a *lot* of things about the life here, Renata, when you allow yourself to – do you know that? It's just that sometimes – *not* sometimes, but *mostly* – you seem to be on the defensive about something. I wonder why?'

She shifted uncomfortably beneath the keenness of his gaze, dropped her eyes to where a few drops of water still glistened amongst the tangle of hair on his teak-brown chest.

'I wouldn't say that.' Rennie made herself sound calmly amused.

'Well, *I* would. You're doing it right now, in fact.' Chad frowned, gave her another level look, and then lapsed into silence once more, lying back and covering his eyes with the hat again. His muscles rippled like brown satin with each movement he made, and Rennie reproached herself as she found herself staring. She was as

143

bad as a gawping schoolgirl!

Presently –

'I hope you won't consider it's been a waste of time, coming to Barrindilloo, Renata? I hope you've enjoyed yourself – *are* enjoying yourself – just a little bit more than you'll admit?'

Rennie glanced away, to where Magda was sitting on a rock, throwing pebbles into the water.

'I won't *regret* having come, Chad, if that's what you mean,' she told him with honesty. 'I'd do it again if I had to – and perhaps much more willingly, knowing it as I do now.' She smiled. 'I think I must have captured Murtie's own philosophy — "I should live the same life over, if I had to live again".'

Beneath the felt brim, Chad's mouth lifted at one corner.

'Adam Lindsay Gordon. The Sick Stockrider,' he informed her lazily. 'It ends up like this –

"Let me slumber in the hollow where the wattle blossoms wave,
With never stone or rail to fence my bed;
Should the sturdy station children pull the bush flowers on my grave,
I may chance to hear them romping overhead." '

'It's nice,' Rennie said shyly.

'Mm. He was our first bush poet. He had a feeling for the Australian scene, even though he wasn't a native. As a matter of fact, he came out from the Mother Country, just like you did yourself.' Chad flicked at the small cloud of flies that were never far away in this heat. 'Not a bad way to end one's life,' he murmured comfortably. 'Especially if the sturdy station children happened to be one's own grandchildren, on one's own station. There's a permanence, a timelessness, about these far-out places, that makes such things quite possible, mere poetry aside.'

His grandchildren. His – and Leith's. There was an odd constriction in Rennie's throat. She got up suddenly.

'I – I think I'll go and see what Magda's doing,' she announced quickly, and then – urgently – 'Chad! She isn't there!'

'Eh?' He was on his feet in an instant. 'Where was she?'

'Just down there, throwing stones from that rock. No, to the left.'

He was already running in the direction Rennie had indicated.

She saw his lean brown frame silhouetted for a moment upon the rock where Magda herself had so recently stood. He seemed to be peering down intently, with immense concentration. Then he lowered himself swiftly into the water, swam several strokes, and duck-dived, disappearing with scarcely a ripple into the cool green depths where a willow drooped its fronds.

When he surfaced he had Magda with him. Rennie watched him bring her up the bank, lay her on the grass face-down, and press his hands firmly on her back.

She found that she was shaking – with relief that the little girl had been found so quickly – with dread, that she might – might—

A whimper sent her speeding down the slope to kneel beside the two figures.

'Oh, Chad! She's—'

'She's O.K.' His deep drawl brought reassurance. Blessed reassurance! 'She's also disobedient,' he added grimly, taking Magda into his arms. 'Didn't I tell you not to dive in that particular pool, Magda? Not *ever*? Because of the snags under the water?'

Chad sounded as if he expected an answer. He sounded – inexorable.

The little girl's face puckered as she nodded, still spluttering and catching her breath in sobs.

'Chad, *don't. Please.*' Rennie's face was ashen, her eyes still huge with fright. 'Here, darling, come to me!'

She tried to reach beyond the muscular brown arms that encircled that childish, shivering body; tried to wrench her precious little Magda from the man who had spoken so harshly. Just for a tiny while, back there lying on the grass, Chad had seemed different, somehow. Companionable, kind. There had been a lingering, indefinable expression in his green eyes that had held some unspoken message that Rennie had been unable to grasp.

Now those same eyes were hard. Implacable. Telling her not to interfere. He was Chad, the tyrant, again.

'Leave her, Renata.'

And as if to echo his command, Magda suddenly wound her arms around his neck and buried her face in his bare chest.

'Oh, Chad, I'm s-sorry.'

'It's all right, pet, you're safe now.'

'I w-won't do it ever again.'

'You'd better *not*!'

Chad was striding ahead swiftly as he was speaking, and after that, Rennie didn't even try to keep up. She followed slowly, unbelievably shaken.

Magda had actually turned away from her! She had turned away from Rennie to Chad – even though he had spoken to her like that! Even though he had spoken to her in that way, in her time of distress it was to him she had turned. Chad had forged a bond of silken delicacy but tensile strength between himself and his little niece – the child of the wild young brother he had loved so much. This man, this child, they understood each other. They didn't need anyone else.

Rennie knew now, knew it for sure, that there was no longer any legitimate reason to keep her at Barrindilloo. The knowledge, instead of delighting her as it should have done, had a curiously depressing effect. Or perhaps it was just reaction after her terrible fright. She needn't feel this way, really, for wasn't Magda already running away, with Chad in mock pursuit, giggling shrilly as he pretended that he couldn't catch her.

As Rennie sank down on to the grass and pulled on her towelling beach-robe that matched the yellow swimsuit, she felt weary to her very bones. A hand came down behind her somewhere, guided her arm into the sleeve of her wrap and pulled the garment up about her shoulders. Chad.

She looked up, smiled her thanks tremulously as she

fastened the sash.

'Take it easy, Renata.' His voice was strangely gruff, and his eyes were watching her face in the way they had done before. Gently, with that same mysterious message. 'It's not the end of the world, you know, so don't tear yourself to pieces over something that didn't happen.'

Her eyes filled unaccountably. She could only gaze at him, wet-lashed, grateful, unable to reply.

'I believe you love that kid, after all, don't you?' he said slowly, on a note of discovery, searching her face with an intent look.

'Of course I love her!' Rennie was indignant now. 'I always *have* loved her, whatever you think of me, Chad. Oh, yes, I know your opinion of me! I suppose you assume it was just to spite you that I didn't want to give her up?'

'And it wasn't?' He grinned suddenly, his eyes quizzical.

'I wanted to see, to assure myself, that this was a suitable home for her to grow up in, that's all,' she replied with dignity, adding in a small voice, 'and I can see now that it is.'

'And what is that supposed to mean?' The green eyes dissected her thoughtfully. They made her want to look away, but she forced herself to meet them unflinchingly.

'Just what I say,' she replied firmly. 'I can realize, now that I've got to know what life is like at Barrindilloo, that Magda will be well cared for here. Better cared for than I could possibly do. She'll settle down all right, regard it as her home. She'll be h-happy.'

There was a tiny break in her voice. Rennie hoped he hadn't noticed it.

Chad turned her towards him, regarded her soberly. She was acutely aware of his hands resting upon her shoulders.

'And what about *you*, Renata?' he asked unexpectedly. 'Could *you* ever come to regard it as your home? Could *you* ever be happy here?'

She? Rennie? What was he *saying*?

There was no place for *her* at Barrindilloo, not with himself and Leith. Leith had already been at pains to point that out, on his behalf as well as her own! Leith and Chad. Keith and Rennie. Rennie minus Magda.

Rennie minus Magda equals Keith. It was like one of those subtraction sums you learned at school!

'I?' she queried lightly, and gave an abrupt laugh which, even to her own ears, sounded unpredictably brittle. 'I don't think I've ever given the question a single thought, since the possibility of my living here is hardly likely to arise, is it?'

And with that, she picked up the little hold-all she had brought and walked quickly after Magda, aware that Chad had remained exactly where he was.

Out of the corner of her eye she could see that his long, brown fingers were stroking his chin as he stood there, looking after her.

CHAPTER EIGHT

The morning of the race meeting dawned clear, accompanied by all the customary inaugural bush sounds that heralded another day.

Chad and Ash had been away for the previous couple of days, preparing in advance for the social invasion that could be expected. They arrived back, tired but satisfied, in the dusty four-wheel-drive Blitz, which had gone out on each of those days laden with supplies, to the site at the Yogill Bore.

'Is everything all right, Ash? Have you done all you have to out there now?'

Rennie could not help sounding excited. The whole homestead seemed to breathe excitement just now, and all hands – except Rennie's – had apparently been needed to do the thousand and one things necessary before all the people arrived.

Rennie, in her innocence, had no idea that already a lot of those people *had* arrived! There were trainers and jockeys out there right now, with strings of horses, and others from surrounding stations and drovers' plants were making their way to the Yogill Bore racetrack with all sorts and descriptions of animals. Each and every rider and trainer who was headed in that direction cherished the secret hope that his own horse was going to win! The air resounded to the echoes of hammers on tent-pegs as the visiting population set about making camp in the surrounding area. The choicest spots were quickly bagged, and the whole place was a buzzing hive of activity. Soon the rush-roofed bar went up, and beside it the canvas-tent 'Tote'. The grandstand and pavilion, the ablutions, the starter's and judges' boxes on the track itself were permanencies that did not need to be erected every year.

When Rennie and the rest of the people from Barrindilloo homestead arrived that day, there was a veritable village of tents, and to her astonishment Chad gravely ushered Rennie to one of her own – or rather, one which she was evidently to share with Leith, and in which the girls would change into their evening dresses for the dance that night.

'You can leave your things there now, Renata. They'll be quite safe. Hang anything up if you want. There are a couple of makeshift hooks there, you see, above those air-beds. It's rough and ready, but the girls always vow it's adequate for all the time they spend here! Close the flap behind you when you come out, though,' he grinned. 'It helps to keep out the dust!'

'Yes, Chad. When do things really begin?'

She stepped out of the tent with him, looked about her in awe.

There were people swarming about everywhere. The women were in their smartest dresses and some sported quite devastating hats, but the men, like Chad himself, appeared to favour the ubiquitous open-necked white shirt with rolled-up sleeves, and moleskins or khaki drills. It was almost a uniform amongst the male fraternity! Bookies were already occupied in calling odds in rusty voices, and outside the Tote a couple of men were writing busily with chalk on a big blackboard.

'The bar, as you can see, has begun to do a brisk trade already, but the first race isn't till one o'clock. He paused, looking down at her in that courteous, yet uncomfortably intent way he had, and seeming to divine her unspoken question, added drily, 'The charter flight from Sydney is due in about half an hour. It lands over there.'

'Oh. Er – thank you.' Rennie blushed.

'Don't mention it.' Chad lifted his hat, walked away.

Rennie stood for a moment outside her tent, eyes drawn with a sort of helplessness from that tall, retreating figure to the place where he had said the flight – *Keith's* flight – would land.

Already there were a number of light aircraft on the ground. It seemed to Rennie's amazed eyes that they were coming in and parking as neatly as if they had been cars! There were cars, too, of course. Every sort of vehicle, in fact, from jeeps and station waggons to battered trucks and gleaming limousines. She marvelled that there could possibly be so many, away out here on this lonely property. So many people, too! Where had they all come from?

She stepped inside the tent again, and proceeded to hang up the frocks she had brought, as Chad had suggested she should. Then she brushed her hair, and went, hatless, out into the sun again to await that plane.

When it arrived, Rennie caught her breath at the sight of the band of sophisticated girls who stepped carefully down. They were without exception elegantly dressed, beautifully groomed. Just for one moment she thought of her own professional wardrobe, back there in the flat with Viv, regretted the simplicity of her button-through linen – and then she forgot all about it, as the men followed the girls from the aircraft, and Keith himself walked towards her. In handsome sophistication, he somehow complemented those pretty girls with whom he had travelled. Rennie had almost forgotten just how handsome, in a marvellously classic and conventional way, Keith was! He wore a light-weight tropic suit whose jacket he carried neatly over one arm, and in his pastel shirt and broad floral tie he was smart, and just a little conspicuous, amongst all those open necks and rolled-up sleeves and country trousers and elastic-sided boots.

Rennie couldn't refrain from smiling at the expression on Keith's face as he looked about him. He was obviously aware of his sartorial superiority, not to say enjoying the fact! Keith was an extrovert. He *liked* to be conspicuous!

He gave her one of those blatantly admiring looks that turned her limbs to jelly, and kissed her.

'Hello, beautiful! I made it, as you can see!'

Over his shoulder, Rennie could see Chad talking to Ash in the shade of a tree nearby. His broad-brimmed hat was pushed to the back of his head, and he was gesturing about something. She was thankful to see that he had now taken a notebook from his hip pocket, and was engaged in jotting something down in it, so it was unlikely that he had even noticed her standing there. She didn't quite know why, but she'd have felt embarrassed if he had happened to see that bold embrace of Keith's. She had discovered that some of these country people had somewhat quaint and old-fashioned ideas about such things! They were – well, almost *reserved*, in a way. They might not understand, or might *mis*understand, an exuberant, extrovert sort of person like Keith, mightn't they? Rennie had no wish to embarrass any of Chad's guests there today.

As she walked contentedly at Keith's side in the direction of some shade also, she saw that a third person had now joined Chad and Ash.

It was Leith. Rennie couldn't actually see her face, because she was wearing a pair of quite enormous sunglasses, but she knew it must be Leith because of the fiery glimmer of deep auburn hair that peeped from under the brim of a pretty cream straw hat. The hat had a band of openly mock fruits clustered around the crown. It was an extravagant hat. Very lovely indeed.

'Now, Rennie, my sweet, we're going to get us a nice cold drink and carry it over to that seat there, and then you're going to tell me how much you've been missing me!'

Keith took her hand and led her in the direction of the makeshift bar.

Once the racing started, the afternoon passed swiftly. There was much laughter and chatter, as people introduced each other, placed bets, leaned on the rails at the track, sat in the stand or at vantage points upon trucks and cars, ate picnics or patronized the barbecue.

The bar was perhaps the busiest and rowdiest place of all. There was a crowd surrounding that particular lean-to shed quite continuously, and several times Rennie caught a glimpse of Murtie's bow-legged figure shambling about its outskirts, beer-can in hand, yarning with his stockman cronies. Once, as she passed by with Keith, he caught her eye and winked, giving her one of those yellow-toothed, rather wickedly leering grins of which he was all too capable.

'Good God! Don't tell me you're on *winking* terms

with the natives! Who's that disreputable character?'

Rennie laughed. 'That's only Murtie. He's a stockman, and he's not disreputable, Keith. He's my friend.'

Keith stared after him, frowning.

'In that case, the sooner you're out of here, the better.'

Rennie glanced at him in some surprise. She had spoken jokingly, but there was no doubting the fact that Keith's eyes were serious, almost accusing.

'Oh, darling, don't be so stuffy! You don't really mean that.'

'Actually, I *do*, Rennie.' He had stopped now, and he was looking down at her in an odd way. 'I *do* mean it, my pet. You seem different, somehow, out here. Not quite *my* Rennie.' He glanced fleetingly at her bare head. 'Where's your hat, by the way, sweetie?'

Rennie put her hand to the top of her bare head, as if to make sure of his question. Her crown felt silky-warm where the sun had been beating down upon it.

'I haven't got one with me,' she confessed, laughing. 'Nothing suitable, that is. Only a beach-hat, and that wouldn't have done – and most of the clothes I brought are too warm to wear. You – you don't *mind*, do you?'

'I suppose not, if you didn't bring one. There was a time, though, Rennie, when you'd have minded *yourself*. When you'd have taken a pride in looking the pick of the bunch, the outstanding girl in the crowd.'

Why, he sounded almost *critical*! Rennie hid her amazement under a gently appeasing smile. Perhaps she hadn't done Keith justice on this occasion, she admitted – faintly miserable – to herself. In her hatless state, in her plain linen shirtwaister, she could hardly be termed the outstanding girl in this particular crowd! But she had to stifle a tiny pang of hurt, all the same, that it should *matter*. After all, she was the same person underneath, wasn't she, even if the clothes she wore did not happen to lead the field today?

She was standing at the rail, watching the fourth successive false start in a line of half-trained, prancing horses, when Ash elbowed his way through the crowd to her side.

'Hullo, Rennie, how goes it? Are you making your fortune?'

Ash looked hot, slightly harassed.

'Not yet, I'm afraid.' Rennie shook her head, smiling. 'And the one I've picked in that present lot seems determined to let me down right at the starting-tape itself!'

The book-keeper chuckled.

'A motley lot, aren't they? Some are old-timers at this game, and do the whole circuit at this time of year. Others aren't so biddable, being simply station horses whose owners are stuck with the idea that they could fluke a win!' He sighed. 'I guess I'm getting too old to be Chad's deputy at this sort of thing. Between finding lost tote tickets for tearful ladies and tent accommodation that isn't here and all the rest of it, I'm beginning to feel the weight of my advancing years.'

'What rubbish, Ash!'

'No, dinkum, Rennie. Chad'll be glad when it's over successfully, too. It's late enough in the season for this sort of thing. We get most of our rain in summer, you know – when we get any, that is! – and he's anxious to muster the Dilloo outstation before the end of the month.'

'Well, it certainly won't rain today, Ash, anyway. Just look at that sky!'

'A good thing it's cloudless, and tomorrow will be, too, by the look of things. Even so, my guess is that they'll be leaving for Dilloo just as soon as possible once it's all over.'

When Ash had left her, Rennie looked about to see if she could see Chad anywhere. She found herself gazing around in search of Leith's pretty cream straw hat, too, but she couldn't seem to see the hat or its owner or Chad anywhere at all. She supposed he must be somewhere behind the scenes organizing something, and very probably Leith would have set herself the voluntary task of helping him.

In the evening there were long queues of people taking turns at the showers. It was marvellous to feel that warmish bore-water cascading down upon one, washing away the dirt and grime. There was no doubt in Rennie's mind that a country race meeting could be an incredibly dusty affair, and by the close of the first day the grounds were soft with a finely churned powder that clung to one's clothes and shoes.

When she returned to the tent, Leith was there, too. She had bathed earlier, and was in the process of making up her face before putting on the evening gown which was hanging up beside Rennie's own. She had brought several additional items with her, Rennie noted, all of which were calculated to bring a more civilized atmosphere to the canvas interior. A battery-powered lamp stood on the butter-box which served as a table, and a narrow mirror had been propped against the rear pole. A polythene bag had been ingeniously nailed-up to do duty as a waste-bin.

'We might as well be as comfortable as possible,' observed Leith with a smile, popping a used tissue into the bag as she spoke. 'When you've been coming to these functions as long as I have, you soon learn to bring a few of the more necessary conveniences along with you!'

That dance in the evening was a happy and informal affair. The main one, Rennie had discovered, was to take place on the second night, to mark the end of the races for another year. She supposed, as she slipped her own dress over her head carefully, that sheer excitement must keep the crowd going for two days and nights, almost non-stop, but as Leith explained, tonight's 'hop' did not go on for as long as the main one, and again the first race would not take place until the afternoon, so one had all the morning to recover from the previous evening's activities.

Rennie checked her appearance in the small mirror as best she could, and then followed the others who were making their way amongst the tents, under the stars, to the place where the music was already sounding.

This evening she wore a cleverly-cut sharkskin dress with a plain, sleeveless top and classically slim, straight skirt. The matt white material showed her smoothly tanned arms to advantage, and the high mandarin collar, heavily jewel-encrusted, was her only adornment. It was a superbly simple gown from one of the world's most famous fashion houses, and was what Rennie secretly termed her 'go-anywhere dress'. As she stepped into the hall, she was satisfied that it looked every bit as correct in an Outback dancing-shed as it might have done at Les Ambassadeurs, and Keith's low whistle verified the fact as he came up immediately to claim her.

'Wow!' was actually all he said, as he was given to doing when something pleased him, but the inflection he gave the word tonight sent a flush of pleasure to Rennie's cheeks. She had not let him down, appearance-wise, this time, at any rate, it seemed!

There were many lovely dresses on view that evening, and many beautiful young women, glowing with health and vigour and vitality and fun in an unselfconscious way that Rennie found peculiarly Australian, and quite refreshingly attractive. Leith Mindon was as beautiful as anyone in that hall, in a way that was subtly different. With her creamy skin and rich auburn hair she stood out amongst her sun-tanned sisters like a frangipanni in a bowl of poinsettias.

There was little noticeable difference about the men's attire compared with what they had been wearing all day, Rennie was amused to see. Admittedly, they had showered too, had changed their shirts and polished the dust off their boots, and some of them had shaved off their five o'clock shadow and slicked their hair down neatly, but essentially the garb remained the same. A sea of sleeve-rolled shirts, some still open-necked, some with a tie now knotted at brown throat as a concession to the added formality of the evening. A mere sprinkling of darker suits.

Rennie danced for the most part with Keith, but from time to time others came up to claim her too. At one point she was seized by the exuberant Murtie, who whirled her off into the crowd with heavy-footed enthusiasm, stamping his feet noisily in time to the Military Two-step which the band had struck up. The go-go sort of dancing which had been the rage when Rennie left home did not appear to have caught on out here, except

156

amongst the youthful visiting contingent, who every now and then succeeded in persuading the orchestra into a more progressive 'beat' rhythm that enabled them to perform their individual interpretations to their evident satisfaction.

'I don't hold with that new-fangled stuff, Renata,' grumbled Murtie loudly, as he stepped heavily on her toe with a pressure that made her flinch. 'What's dancin' for, if it ain't ter get a sheila cuddled up in yer arms, I'd like ter know? I reckon that other's real silly, if you arst me! More like limberin' up fer a karate session than proper dancin', I reckon!'

'Er – quite, Murtie,' Rennie felt bound to admit, sensing that she would be the loser in any discussion that might ensue over this particular topic.

Some time later, the band really let itself go in a manner which no doubt would have brought a scowl of disapproval to Murtie's lined features had Rennie been able to espy him at that moment amongst the crowd. She wasn't actually *trying* to look for Murtie, though, because her eyes were drawn unwillingly, like most other people's, to the couple at one corner of the floor who were performing this particular number in a way that merited attention and admiration, however reluctantly given.

Leith Mindon was the girl – a slender, gyrating, athletic, graceful figure, she was moving her body with a frenzied accuracy of beat, an impassioned rhythm that was appealing, sensuous and *riveting*. She was an accomplished mistress of this particular art form, and she knew it, revelled in it. She hadn't a rival in the whole room, and she knew that, too.

So did the other dancers. One by one they left the floor, propped themselves idly against the wall, watching. Even the other girls' faces betrayed grudging admiration. The men, almost without exception, were enthralled.

'Leith's at her thing again.' Rennie heard a masculine murmur from somewhere behind her. 'Just look at that, will you? There's no one to touch her when it comes to this!'

Or her companion either. Rennie was unsurprised that it

was Chad himself, but his skill at this particular activity caused her a secret pang of envy for the girl who had found such a partner to accompany her in what now amounted to a quite devastating performance. Chad's own part in it was restrained, understated, as though acknowledging Leith's claim to the limelight. He was simply acting as a foil for her own impassioned exhibition, and a very successful foil he was! With his fair head thrown back, white teeth gleaming in his dark face, he was encouraging the girl by each clap of his brown hands, each movement of his sinuous, athletic body, as clearly as if he were actually saying to her 'This is *your* show, my girl! Now let them see what you can do!'

When the music stopped, a round of wild applause broke out, and there were chorused entreaties for more. Chad gave an amused, half-sheepish grin, shook his head, handed Leith over to the crowd who had surged around her, and walked across the floor to talk to the bandleader, after which Rennie saw him going off with Ash once more. It was only shortly after that that she felt a tap on her shoulder and, turning, saw that Chad was back.

He was standing right beside her, and when she looked up at him, he smiled.

'May I have this dance, Renata, please?' he asked, and without waiting to see what she would say, he took her by the elbow and guided her firmly on to the floor.

Chad did not try to show Rennie off to the crowd in the way in which he had done with Leith. Instead, he took her into an impersonally conventional hold and began to waltz her around slowly, amongst the other couples. He did not attempt to speak, and Rennie, glancing up with sudden unaccountable shyness, saw that he was in fact looking over the top of her head without expression. It was all too obvious that this was merely a duty dance, and that he had invited her to do it out of pure politeness.

Chad was a superb dancer, she had seen that already during that exhibition with Leith. Rennie felt as though she were floating on air. Their steps matched perfectly as hey whirled slowly around to this dreamy, nostalgic tune. It was an old, familiar melody, one that Rennie had known for years – unashamedly sentimental, sad and lilting. A *forever* sort of tune. The lights had gone down now, to a pinkish glow, and Rennie felt Chad's arms tightening imperceptibly about her, drawing her closer. She felt his hand upon her back, moving up, bringing her right against his clean white shirt, and surprisingly, she had no wish, no will, to resist. There was a tiny catch in her throat, a feeling of pain about her heart that made her suddenly yearn for this moment to go on for ever, for time to stand still. It was scarcely less than an exquisite, unbearable agony, as she melted against him. His fingers tightened over hers, his breath was warm on her cheek. They were swaying slowly together, in time to that soft, sad music – two people fused into one, bound in some sort of indefinable magic that brought Chad's head right down beside hers so that his lips were near her own. They were not set in that punishing, calculating line, those lips, not now, not this time. They were parted just a little bit, curving tenderly, just as his eyes seemed strangely tender, gentle, as she found her gaze irresistibly drawn to his in that soft, dim light. Tender. Questioning.

'My girl, I think, Sandasen.' Keith's voice broke in. 'I've been looking everywhere for you, Rennie. Couldn't find you in this blasted gloom! I thought this was supposed to be our dance.' He sounded injured, annoyed.

'Yes, of course. I – I'm sorry, Keith, I *did* look—'

Dazed by the emotion that had taken possession of her, bewildered, confused, Rennie felt herself transferred from one man's arms to the other's. And then, with a curt nod, the briefest of bows, Chad had gone, and she was being whisked away by Keith instead.

The remainder of that evening passed for Rennie in a state of suspended animation. She could not afterwards have said what she had done, to whom she had spoken, with whom she had danced. She only knew that Chad did not come back. Nor did he speak to her again that night, and when she met his eyes, just once, across the room, they were unrevealing, his features remote and stern. She knew then that she had imagined that tenderness, that magical feeling of togetherness, of completeness, as his arm had tightened about her, drawing her close to him. The music, the soft lights, the nostalgic, lilting refrain, had had some sort of temporary, crazy effect upon her sanity that Rennie had been quite powerless to control. It had nothing to do with Chad himself, of course it hadn't! And yet it must have had *something* to do with him, because – back in Keith's arms – the feeling had vanished.

All through the next day she found her gaze irresistibly drawn in the direction of Chad's rugged, sunbrowned face, searching for some clue as to why he had made her feel that way last night. He seemed busier than ever today, and he didn't stop to speak for long when she finally found herself talking to him, although his manner was courtesy itself, even if it was that cool sort of politeness which he seemed to have decided to reserve especially for her. All the others to whom he spoke appeared to be receiving the full impact of his particular charm, the lopsided smile, the laughter that crinkled the green eyes into teasing slits.

Only Rennie did not.

Never mind, perhaps he would ask her to dance again this evening, and she would then discover that magical mood once more. She might even be able to identify the question those lazy green eyes had been asking.

To her disappointment Chad did not invite her to dance at all. Even when Keith took the floor with Leith, as he did on several occasions, Chad never even looked her way.

When Keith returned to her side, he was smiling.

'Sorry to desert you, sweetie, but that little sugar-plum is hard to resist. Do you think that auburn hair is the real thing, or out of a bottle?'

'It's real, I'm sure, Keith,' she replied, somehow – inexplicably – irritated all of a sudden. 'Does it matter?'

'Not a bit,' he replied cheerfully. 'It's quite gorgeous, whichever it is.' He glanced down at her. 'Tut, tut! We're not jealous, are we?'

Rennie allowed herself to be led on to the floor half-heartedly. She couldn't think what was the matter with her! She felt no joy at Keith's nearness, no pleasure in his company tonight. She found herself almost wishing that he had gone back to Leith again, that he had left her alone with this miserable, unhappy listlessness which seemed to have taken possession of her this evening.

Over his shoulder she could see Chad's tall form, wide-shouldered in the crisp white shirt and narrow trousers. He was dancing with a plump, elderly woman who had a plain, almost ugly face, and a tight frizz of blue-rinsed hair. Her dress was over-exposed, unbecomingly youthful, although it might have looked nice upon someone half her age. Chad's fair head was bent down, a little to one side, as he listened gravely to what the woman was saying, his eyes intent. All night long he had been carrying out his duties as host with impeccable impartiality, although Leith Mindon herself could probably claim with some legitimacy to have had more dances with him than anyone else. He had asked almost all the girls in turn, and now he was dancing with that plump, over-made-up dowager, and he was turning on the full measure of his charm in exactly the same way as he had done with those attractive younger girls. With everyone, in fact, except Rennie herself.

'I wish the band would zip things up a bit,' complained Keith forcibly as he twirled her around several times on a double beat. 'I don't think our little redhead likes it much either. She's not doing her stuff over there at all!'

'Isn't she?'

Now Chad was speaking, replying to what the woman had been saying. Rennie could see his expression softening, the corner of his mouth curving into a slow smile as he murmured something into the woman's ear. And then they were both laughing, spontaneously, gaily, and the woman was blushing almost coyly. And it was then that Rennie noticed that she wasn't plain at all, that woman – not really. A little homely, yes, maybe, but not ugly, not plain, because as she laughed so pleasedly at whatever Chad had said, her eyes were soft and glowing, and her cheeks were flushed and girlish, and there was a warmth in her expression, a pleasure, a sincerity, that lifted her out of the realms of mere ordinariness, that made her, suddenly, quite beautiful with happiness.

The same warmth and pleasure and sincerity were reflected in Chad's own features just then, in the affectionate laughter still lingering in his eyes, in the tender curve still lifting his mouth into a smile, in the very way he suddenly twirled his elderly partner around in a youthful pirouette and started listening to what she was saying all over again with his former grave, patient attention.

And it was in that moment that Rennie realized that she loved him.

She loved Chad Sandasen, with every fibre of her being. Loved him, quite *passionately*, for the very qualities she had just been witnessing, all the qualities that Keith did not – could never – possess. She loved him for his charm that was there for everyone, not just turned on and off for special people, a charm of which he wasn't even aware. Loved him for his patience, his forbearance, his quiet courtesy, his unfailing considerateness, his sincerity, his kindness to a plump and plain old woman who had turned into a happily beautiful one just because he had bent his tanned, sun-fair head and murmured something into her ear – something nice, it must have been, something that gave her genuine pleasure. Rennie loved him for those other things too – the things that had so irked her, the things she had fought so hard against. His sense of purpose, the authority which he had dared her to question, his self-assurance, his perceptiveness, his ability to govern, to organize, to rule.

She knew, quite suddenly, quite positively, that she wouldn't mind being ruled, being governed, by Chad. Not *now*. Not when she loved him like this!

She pulled herself up with a start, came back to reality with a bump – right back into Keith's arms. The *wrong* arms.

Rennie looked about her in acute, almost uncontrollable panic. There were people everywhere, milling about and around her. Young and old. Fair and dark.

Happy people. Gay people. Friendly people. Shy people. Polished people. Uncouth people. People who laughed and chatted as they danced, drank, talked, ate. And there was Rennie – alone – on a small private island of misery because of the shattering discovery which she had just made about herself.

She collected herself with an effort. They mustn't guess! Not any of them! Least of all *him*! He was too good at guessing what people were thinking and feeling, but this was one occasion upon which he was going to have no opportunity of doing so, she must see to that!

Rennie did see to it forthwith.

She was gay, brittle, amusing, talkative. She kept up that façade of laughter and fun and high spirits so successfully that Keith, gratified, did not even bother to slide his eyes towards Leith's bobbing red head any more, as he had surreptitiously been doing all evening, but kept them upon Rennie's own animated face in the old absorbed and fascinated way.

She kept it up successfully, that façade, for the whole of the rest of the night – an interminable night. She even succeeded in keeping it up next morning as she stood with Chad and Ash, who were waiting to drive her back to the homestead, and waved goodbye to Keith as he stepped aboard the charter plane once more.

'See you soon, Rennie!' He blew her a kiss from the step.

'Yes, soon! *Soon!*' she answered, and there were tears in her eyes because of the enormous effort she had had to make, tears because of the futility beneath her pretence, tears because of the emptiness inside her.

Chad saw those tears shimmering on her lashes, she knew, because he was watching her quite intently at the time, but he made no comment, simply resettled his broad-brimmed hat a little lower over his eyes, and held open the door of the Blitz for her to climb in.

Overhead, the plane droned off into the blue. Below, the last of the cars were leaving the Yogill Bore, straggling away over the plain again in the varying directions from whence they had come. His passengers safely installed, the last of the gear stowed, the litter and debris cleared away, Chad started the engine, let in the clutch, and drove back to Barrindilloo in silence.

Rennie was quiet, too, and Ash had gone to sleep. When the Blitz clanked noisily over the cattle-grid near the homestead, he stirred, opened his eyes, sat forward once more and yawned.

'Well, Chad, that's it over for another year, eh? A success, I reckon, by any standards.'

'I expect so, Ash.' Chad sounded curiously abrupt. As if he wanted to forget all about the race meeting, put it behind him for keeps.

At the house he leapt out, went around to the rear of the vehicle and began unloading things with a sort of maniacal energy.

Magda came racing down the steps, yelling excitedly.

'Chad! Rennie! You're back! Oh, Ash, you've all been gone *ages*!'

'Two whole days,' Ash grinned into her accusing face, tweaked her fair hair away from her forehead casually. 'How've you been?'

Elspeth had followed hot on the heels of her small charge. A glance from Chad's set, absorbed face as he carried things inside, to Rennie's unusual pallor, made her exclaim,

'Lands' sakes, you look dead beat, the lot of you! I'll rustle up some tea straight away!'

Tea was evidently Elspeth's panacea for all ailments. It was good, too, that tea. Rennie gulped hers down gratefully.

After lunch she retired to her room to hang up her dresses and put away the few things she had taken with her. She was trying hard not to think. She concentrated woodenly upon what she was doing right now with quite unnecessary attention to detail, smoothed out the jewelled collar of the white sharkskin frock, rearranging it again on the hanger, tidying each drawer as she put things away with mechanical precision.

It was no good, though, was it, pretending like this? Pretending that there wasn't anything to think about?

That things were still the same as before? They weren't the same, and they never could be again, and that was something that had to be faced, had to be recognized, had to be thought about! Yes, clearly Rennie must somehow find the courage to look at her problem with honesty. If she could bring herself to do that, she might find a solution, shape some fresh plans for her future.

Not here, though. She couldn't think about it here.

A sudden desperate need for complete solitude sent her back to the dressing-chest to find her jeans. She dragged them on, tucked in a shirt, slipped her feet into canvas plimsolls, put on her beach-hat and went down to the yards.

The selection of station horses wasn't up to much today. Nothing as exciting or challenging as that handsome black rogue. She saddled up a passable-looking bay gelding, led him out, and swinging up on to his back, cantered away.

He had a pleasant way with him, an easy pace, that old station horse, but today Rennie hardly noticed. She dug her heels in, spurred him to a gallop, as if she and he could simply gallop away into the distance, far from all her problems, leaving them all behind.

The distance became the present, the first horizons were behind her, as new vistas stretched in front. Together they thudded over the plain, in and out of the stands of mulga, over the winding channels of greener vegetation flanked by the sturdy boles of the ghost-gums which told one that these were the water-ways when the rains came. It didn't look like rain just now, though, if you discounted those few rather leaden-looking clouds that had gathered away to the left. Rennie hadn't seen a cloud for days, but the few that did appear always floated away again into the west, to become a part of those rosy, woolly sunsets which, out here, were always so breathtakingly lovely.

Since the last dry channel had been crossed, the country had changed. It was wilder, rougher, sand-ridged, gibberstrewn. Clumps of spinifex clung to the barren earth, and steely balls of roly-poly went scattering over the sand as a sudden breeze lifted them before it. The sight of them rolling crazily along in front of her horse brought Rennie's mind back to her present whereabouts. She had come far enough. Too far, probably. Her horse was heaving, foam-flecked. She must have been mad not to have noticed how tired he was!

She dismounted at a stand of timber, tied the reins to a mulga branch where the animal could rest in the shade, and found herself a seat on a fallen log. About her there was utter stillness, save for the quiet champing of the horse and the twittering exchanges of a pair of honey-eaters that darted about in the sparse blossoms above her head.

Alone with her thoughts, Rennie forced herself to turn things over in her mind. She must come to grips with herself, because after all, one had to go on living, didn't one, even if the implications were unpleasantly plain? Her future stretched far before her, barren, empty, because it couldn't possibly include the one person who could alleviate that barrenness, that emptiness. Chad. For Chad belonged to Leith Mindon. And Leith belonged to Chad.

And even Magda belonged to Chad, now, too. And Rennie didn't belong to anybody. Not to *anybody*.

Rennie minus Magda *didn't* equal Keith, at all. Something had gone wrong with that comforting equation. It just didn't add up any more. Rennie could never go to Keith now, even without Magda, knowing that she was in love – irreparably, irrevocably in love! – with another man.

No, Rennie minus Magda didn't equal Keith. It simply equalled loneliness and heartache and the years stretching away, away, away, having to be got through somehow, all by oneself, without Keith whom she didn't love, without Chad whom she *did*.

What a bleak, bleak prospect!

A shadow came over the sun just as she reached that inevitable, inescapable conclusion, a shadow of gloom that darkened the sky and deepened the shade in amongst the thin, gaunt trees about her. The air was heavy, hot, dust-laden, oddly oppressive. The stillness was complete. There was no sound anywhere, not even the quiet chink of the horse's bit or the soft twittering of the honey-eaters.

And then the sky got darker, and looking up, Rennie noticed for the first time its leaden grey appearance, the sullen clouds that hung low over the mulga. And at the same moment there came a long, slow grumbling from up there in the sulky grey clouds, followed almost instantly by a shattering explosion of sound. As a blinding bolt of lightning followed the unexpected thunderclap, and then another reverberating bang, she heard a shrill neigh of terror, saw the old bay gelding rear wildly away from the tree where he had been tied and gallop off, trailing his broken rein after him into the scrub.

Oh, no! Now what was she to do?

Rennie watched helplessly as he disappeared from view. She scrambled to her feet, followed the direction he had taken, calling quietly. Stupidly, she realized that she did not even know the horse's name.

'Here, boy! Here, boy!'

It was useless. The hoof-beats had died away. There was nothing for it but to start walking home.

With the disappearance of the sun, it was hard to tell the time, but Rennie judged that it could only be about mid-afternoon. She would easily make the homestead before dark, even if it started to rain, which it looked as though it might easily do! She could see that already one of those rainclouds was shedding its burden away in the far-off distance, by the way it lost its roundness and became a streaked grey shape connecting vertically with the horizon itself. Shafts of sunlight filtered weakly through its sodden, lessening barrage, and within an hour the sun had spread again to the place where Rennie was, beating down relentlessly upon her as she trudged. Almost she wished that the rain had happened here, for, walking like this, the heat was well-nigh unbearable, and a cloud of tiny flies tormented her persistently as she dragged her dusty feet along through patches of sand and dry grass, over gibber, amongst prickly spinifex.

Some time later, making wearily for a stand of timber and some welcome shade, Rennie felt the first faint twinge of panic, the first tenuous flutter of alarm. It was the same mulga wood that she had set out from, all those miles ago! There was the very log upon which she had sat, there was the broken branch of the very tree to which she had tied up the horse!

Rennie sat down on the log again, bewildered. How could she possibly have arrived back here, when she had been walking *away* all the time?

Her forehead was wet with perspiration, and her shirt clung to her back in sticky patches, and the flies clung to the shirt. The soles of her feet were burning, and her throat was dry, parched with dust, tight with the first tenseness of real fear.

She forced herself to be calm. What she should have done in the first place was to leave little landmarks as she went, so that she couldn't possibly double up on her tracks. And if she kept the sun in the same position in relation to herself all the time, allowing for a little variation because of the hours passing, she was bound to be all right. It was understandable, the way she must have got confused, for all these mulga stands looked much alike, and there was a drab sameness about the vast country that stretched interminably about her.

After that, Rennie walked carefully. Every now and then she checked her position, and as she went she broke little twigs, placed stones, heaped tussocks of grass, to show herself that she was breaking fresh ground all the time.

It was as dusk was falling and she was literally staggering with weariness and thirst and hunger, that she came upon one of her own little signs. Rennie stared disbelievingly at the pale, sappy place where she had ripped and broken the tiny twig, and sank down weakly at the root of that twisted tree.

She was lost.

Darkness fell in a swift, blanketing cloak, the way it did out here. Huddled under the shelter of that gnarled trunk, Rennie slept only fitfully, shivering as the air cooled to a degree she could scarcely have believed possible. She could hardly wait for daylight, and as soon as she could see she began to walk again. She walked and walked, staggering along under the blazing sun. The hunger pangs which had tormented her last night were there no longer. All she felt was a gnawing, hollow pain in her stomach, but she was consumed by a raging thirst that grew now with every yard she trudged. It was a slow, ever-present torture, that thirst. By noon she began to imagine the cool trickle of water running down her parched throat. She kept seeing little lakes of the stuff, pools that shimmered and beckoned. When she reached them there was nothing there, just sand that stung her eyes, and stones that bruised her knees, and spiny spinifex that tore at her clothes and scratched at her hands as she crawled away from where the pools had been, and got slowly to her feet again. Her vision blurred as she swayed where she stood for a moment, and then forced herself on.

Moving had become a real effort now. She had no reserves of strength left. Even breathing was difficult, for her throat was rasping, her lips cracked and swollen, her tongue stiff and numb.

Ahead of her there was a line of trees, or had she imagined that, too?

No, she hadn't – surely? They were there in front of her very eyes, a threading row of white-butted gums that flanked a winding route of darker, greener vegetation. It was the dried-up creek-bed over which Rennie had galloped on her way from the homestead. Or, if it wasn't the same one, it was very like it. It didn't matter, anyway. There would be water there. A soak. Murtie had told her that if you dug down you would find it. That was all that mattered just now. Water.

She began to run, with a sudden energy born of sheer desperation, and then she tripped headlong over a stone, went down heavily, wrenching her foot as she did so. The pain in her ankle made her want to cry out. She would have cried out if she could, but only a little croaking sound came, torn from her as she fell forward.

Before Rennie opened her eyes the next time, she could

feel the sun searing her eyelids. Her hat was lying a little way away. Painfully she eased herself the few feet necessary to retrieve it, lay back thankfully, and put it over her nose. She had seen the line of trees again, but she couldn't be bothered to even think about them. They were too far away, and Rennie knew it. She didn't much care what happened now, because she had no fight, no spunk, left in her.

This was the way Chad had put his hat over his face and lain back, that day on the river-bank, just the way she had hers now. Only his hat was wider, of course, and made of felt. It wasn't a rather silly, pretty little beach-hat, with a floppy, stitched brim and daisies around the crown. She half giggled at the thought of Chad in a hat like *that*! She could see his face quite clearly, tanned and weathered, with those steady, clear green eyes and that level mouth and squared-off jawline and the fine, seamed scar that ran right down from his ear to his shirt collar. She could remember the way his mouth had looked, that day, with the hat covering the rest of his face, too, could remember the way it had lifted at the corners from under the hat, as he had lazily finished off that quotation for her, the one Murtie had begun.

'Let me slumber in the hollow where the wattle blossoms wave,
With never stone or rail to fence my bed.'

Well, there were certainly no rails here, and no fences either. And no wattle-trees, come to that, not so far as she could recall. She was quite sure, if she could be bothered to lift her head, that the only trees out here were those ones along the creek-bed, and they were not even in blossom.

No rails, no fences, no wattle-blossom.

Just sun and dust and stones.

Nothing else, unless you included those crows up there, circling around, cawing so eerily. *Go away!* Rennie removed the hat from her face, waved it weakly at them, and then, when they took no notice, replaced it philosophically upon her nose again. Although she knew that they were there, she didn't have to look at them, did she? No one could *make* her look at them, not if she didn't want to!

She was wondering dreamily to herself what Chad would have done about those crows when she thought she heard voices, and there were the crows, rising up higher into the air and flying away, so they must have thought they heard them, too. Silly birds! You'd think they'd have realized there couldn't be voices away out here! Only *her* voice, that is. She opened her mouth and tried to use it, but this time she couldn't even croak.

After that, Rennie closed her eyes and gave up thinking, simply because it was too much trouble.

CHAPTER NINE

'MIGHT be her finish, Boss.'

'You bring water, quickfella, Harry.'

'T'inkit youngfella missus bin walkabout too-much longtime, not catchem tucker, not catchem water. Might-be her finish. Deadfella.'

'That prop'ly rubbish, Harry! You get water, plurry quick.'

'You-ai, Chad.'

Rennie opened her eyes.

If that really *was* Chad, and he got all angry and narky like he had when she fell off the black horse, Rennie would never forgive him! And if he started asking stupid questions, or reading lectures, or saying things – things like 'I told you so' – she wouldn't forgive him for that, either! She would just close her eyes again and die right here, *dead*fella, where she was lying, and that would teach him a lesson!

When she looked at the head looming above hers, shutting out the sun, she saw that it was indeed Chad's. But he didn't say 'I told you so'. And he didn't seem angry, either. His face was pale, sallow under its heavy tan, but although it was grim and set, it was patient rather than angry.

He was bathing her mouth and lips and tongue with water out of his hat. It seemed a funny place to have water, but that's where it was, and he was dipping a white linen handkerchief into the hat and then squeezing it gently over her mouth, so that it ran down the side of her chin and on to her neck.

Rennie didn't mind, because it was a cool, pleasant feeling. She wished that she could swallow some of the water, but she felt too weak to worry. Maybe, in fact, the water wasn't even there. Maybe Chad wasn't, either. Maybe they were just illusions, mirages, like those shimmering lakes and pools that had sent her staggering on over the plain to scrabble fruitlessly in the sand.

She closed her eyes again wearily. If they were illusions, the sooner she forgot about them the better.

'Killem dat leg, too, Boss.'

'A sprain, Harry, that's all. Not badfella, that-one. More better we get her drinking first. You lift her head up now, eh?'

Rennie's mind was confused, but she swallowed instinctively, just in case it really *was* water that was trickling slowly into her mouth. She went on drinking it until someone said she's had enough, and then she felt herself lifted up, too tired even to see whose were the arms that carried her, Harry's or Chad's. They were strong arms, firm as a rock, but the movement itself made her more light-headed than ever.

A rushing, bubbling sound made her look down fleetingly in panic. They seemed to be wading now, she and her rescuer, through knee-deep, swirling brown water. The same trees were there in their sentinel lines, the trees that had flanked the dry water-course, only now it wasn't dry at all. It was covered up, all the dark green vegetation, by a shallow, rushing, wide brown stream, and only the trunks of the trees were showing. Their bases were hidden under a bubbling froth.

How could it possibly be full of water, that creek-bed, when she knew perfectly well that it was dry? She closed her eyes against the sight of the giddying current. She must be dreaming it, the rushing noise, the arms that were holding her safely above it. She must be dreaming about water again! *Lots* of water!

'Keep still, Rennie. Lie still, darling.'

The arms tightened around her, and lips brushed her forehead, coaxing her into quietness.

So it wasn't Chad who was there after all. Not Chad. Not Harry. But Keith.

It must be Keith, because he was the only person who ever called her 'Rennie' and 'darling'. With Chad it was always 'Renata', and *never* that other word. *Never* 'darling'. It was Keith who was holding her, after all, and she didn't want it to be Keith. She didn't love Keith. She never could, not now, so she mustn't let him go on holding her so closely. She mustn't let him go on thinking – thinking—

'Keith,' she murmured, and pushed at the broad chest – and he must have heard her, for after that there was only the sound of the water, no more voices at all.

Rennie had but the vaguest memories of that journey back to Barrindilloo homestead in the Blitz. Chad was there again, and he gave her another drink from the metal water-can he kept in the back. When they reached the house, he carried her inside to her room, and called Elspeth to help her to undress and lie between the sheets. She wanted to laugh, because his arms had been so taken up with carrying her that he hadn't been able to remove his hat. Chad *always* took his hat off whenever he stepped in through the gauze door on to the veranda, but today it was still right down over his eyes as he laid her on the coverlet. Rennie smiled because it was funny. She thought Chad might have seen the joke too, but he didn't give her an answering smile at all, not even a tiny one. Instead, he looked soberly at her, put his fingers on her wrist and waited there a moment, and then he went away. When he came back, he had removed the hat, and he had brought two different lots of tablets and some more water. He helped Rennie to a sitting position and made her start swallowing all over again, after which he attended to her bruised ankle.

'Now, Renata, Elspeth will bring you a cup of tea, and then you'll be able to sleep. Does that feel more comfortable?'

'Yes, thank you.'

She smiled again, and this time there was the tiniest, answering smile from Chad. He looked around for his hat, remembered it wasn't there, shrugged at his own forgetfulness with another faint smile, and left the room.

Rennie had to admit that, after that, they were all of them kindness itself.

After Elspeth's tea, she gave way to the pleasant sense of drowsiness and well-being that had stolen over her, and slept.

She slept for a long time, and then just off and on. Sometimes it was dark, and sometimes it was light.

When she woke up properly, Magda was sitting at the table beside her bed with a jigsaw puzzle spread out in front of her. She had completed the border of the picture, and now she was working towards the middle, her tongue protruding as she concentrated laboriously over her task.

'The blue bit there belongs to the woman's dress, don't you think?' prompted Rennie helpfully, leaning first upon one elbow, and then bringing herself upright and swinging her legs over the edge of the bed.

'Oh, hullo, Rennie. You're awake again!' The child scraped her chair back eagerly. 'Ash said I was to tell him when you woke up.'

'No need, poppet. I'll get dressed and go along to see him myself. I'm feeling fine now, I really am. As good as I ever was!'

She was, too. Quite back to normal. She tested her weight on the lightly bandaged ankle and was pleased to find that it did not pain her any longer.

'I'd better get him, all the same. Elspeth's gone to feed the hens.' Magda sounded anxious. Her eyes were round with a sense of responsibility.

'No, don't do that, Magda. Look, I'm as right as pie now. I could dance and sing and skip, if it would show you, but they'd probably think me too silly for words if they heard me!' She took a few tentative paces, relieved to find that she could walk quite normally, without the lightheadedness that had plagued her before, although she still felt a little weak.

'Ash wouldn't think you were silly. He's been awful worried.'

'Awfully, not awful,' corrected Rennie automatically. 'Has he? Been worried, I mean? I'm sorry, darling. What a lot of bother I've caused, haven't I?'

'Well—' Magda hesitated – 'it wasn't Ash who had the bother, anyway, Rennie, so he won't be angry with you, even if I do tell him, see.'

She gave Rennie a cherubic, comforting, blandly innocent smile.

But there were implications in that innocent assurance of little Magda's, weren't there? And the implication, surely, was that *someone* was angry, or had been angry, even if it hadn't been Ash. And the someone who was most likely to have been angry was the someone who had had the bother. And, thinking in that logical way, her reasoning brought her back to Chad.

'Was he *very* angry – Chad?' she asked the little girl directly. She might as well know the worst!

Magda stood up and put her feet together and her hands at the sides of her red cotton shorts, as if she were about to recite a lesson – and in a way that was just what she *was* about to do!

'*Chad* says,' she began importantly, 'that if *I'm* ever bushed, the right thing to do is to stay in one place. Chad says I'm to stay right there and wait, because he and Harry can follow my tracks and find out where I've gone. He said the rain nearly beat them, and washed some of your tracks away, see, and it was a while before they could pick them up again, and that's how they didn't find you quicker. But he said if you'd stayed where you were, it wouldn't have taken them nearly so long, and you'd have been in better shape. That's what he said – in better *shape*. And Chad said while you're staying where you are and keeping in good shape you can send out a signal, like lighting a fire or something if you're a grown-up and if you're careful, very careful, where you do it, and then they'll see the smoke, see? And if you *aren't* a grown-up, you just stay there, and every now and then you holler, good and loud. And Chad said, even that way, just sitting there, he and Harry'd most certainly find you. Chad said there are all sorts of things you can do, too, if you know how, like getting grubs to eat from under the bark, and water from a horrible frog that carries it about inside him, and digging down at the channel-beds where everything looks greenest, only you may have to dig quite deep, and Chad says that even putting a pebble in your mouth and sucking it helps, because it keeps the sal – sal – what was the word he said again?—'

Rennie could scream! She would, if she stayed here a minute longer, listening to all the things Chad said she should have done!

'I'm going to shower and freshen up,' she interrupted Magda brightly, fastening her kimono over her pyjamas as she spoke. 'And after that I'll dress, and we'll go and tell Ash I'm up.'

She put on her pretty lemon shift with the white saddle-stitching, and spent a long while brushing the tangles out of her long, straight blonde hair, and then she spent some more time – quite a *bit* more time – in making up her face, rougeing away the unnatural pallor that lingered as a result of her recent experience. She wanted to be looking her best, her prettiest, in order to face Chad. The knowledge that she was looking just as beautiful as possible would help to give her confidence. It would act as a defence against his possible ire, because there was every chance that he might still be very angry. That was why she took so long, winged her brows with the tiny comb, painted in her pale rose mouth with extra care, darkened her curling lashes with her brown mascara-applicator, smoothed and shaped her nails where they had become ragged from groping in the sand, tinted them with pearly-pale varnish. A tiny dab of perfume at ears and throat, and Rennie decided that she was ready.

She stepped out of her room on to the veranda, and then walked along it, around the corner, to Ash's office. He was there, as she had guessed he might be, surrounded by the usual pile of papers, letters, documents. He looked up in surprise as she entered, and then his eyes kindled with genuine pleasure as he came over and took her hands in his.

'Rennie, how good to see you up!' He gave her an almost paternal inspection. 'How do you feel now, my dear? Better? I must say you *look* it, anyway.'

'Much, much better, Ash – quite myself again, thanks. I – I'm terribly sorry to have been such a nuisance.'

'Not a nuisance, Rennie, but we *were* very anxious about you.' He placed a chair for her. 'We won't even talk about it, though. Try to put the whole experience right behind you, and forget about it. It really is pleasing to see you fully recovered!' He beamed at her. 'Elspeth will be as glad as I am that you are on your feet again. Chad, too, when he comes back.'

'Back? You mean, in for tea?'

Rennie felt a tiny sag of disappointment that Chad was not actually about the homestead, when she had groomed herself for the meeting she was half dreading, half longing for. What a painful thing one-sided love could be, when you were prepared to accept even the humblest crumb of attention from the loved one with a gratitude that was out of all proportion to what you could expect to receive! That's how it was with her! The merest glimpse was better than no sight of him at all, the possible lecture she might receive was better than no word!

'No, not for tea. He's away.'

'Away?' Rennie blinked.

'That's right. Probably for another ten days or so.' Ash lit a cigarette, leaned back. 'You remember,' he continued conversationally, 'I mentioned it to you before your – er – illness. Perhaps you'd forgotten. They're mustering the Dilloo Outstation. The men are all out there, and Chad followed just as soon as he'd brought you in the other day.'

'Oh.' Rennie blinked again. It was hard to take in what Ash had just told her, hard to believe that Chad had simply dumped her on her bed and *gone away*, that he hadn't even waited to see if she would recover, that he cared so *little*!

She had gone quite pale as she leaned back limply in the chair, scarcely able to accept what she had just heard. A good thing she had put on that blush-tint and the lip-stick, for she knew the colour had drained right out of her cheeks.

Ash, luckily, didn't seem to notice.

'Yes,' he was saying, 'Elspeth and Magda and I have all been keeping an eye on you, taking turns, since Chad left. Fortunately, these were just scattered thunderstorms that time. They brought a couple of creeks down a banker, but they won't have interfered with the muster, and we were needing the rain badly, even though Chad and Harry were cursing it at the time they were out looking for you. But there—' Ash stood up – 'we aren't going to talk about that any more, are we? Come and we'll find Elspeth, and let her know the patient is completely mended!'

She managed a wan smile, followed him obediently, but, inside herself, she was crying. Just a lost object that had to be found before he could get on with the job in hand – that's all she meant to Chad, that was all he thought of her! She felt belittled, humiliated, hurt beyond words. She felt *cheap*. Ashamed of herself and the way she had prettied herself up just now, in a pitiful bid to catch the attention, earn the admiration, of a man who thought so little of her as *that*! Oh, Rennie, where is your pride? How much lower can you sink?

'Eat up, Rennie. You're just picking at your food.'

'I'm sorry, Elspeth. It's delicious, truly. It's just that I'm not hungry.'

'You're still looking peaky, I reckon.' That was Ash, chiming in.

They meant well, she knew that, but their solicitous attitude only increased her misery.

Rennie stuck it for three days, and then she admitted the truth. She couldn't go on like this. Couldn't bear the thought of seeing Chad again, knowing how little she meant to him. If she had to go, she'd rather go *now*. In fact, it was imperative that she go now, before he came back at all, otherwise her heart might break right up into little splintered fragments, and she might never manage to put the pieces together again. And she couldn't afford such a thing as that to happen, because there were all those years and years to be got through, to be lived out somehow, without Chad. Seeing him again was only going to turn the knife, cause fresh agony. At least she could save herself that! She couldn't go on grovelling like this to be noticed, when all the time it had been made clear to her that he was in love with another woman!

In Ash's office once more, she couldn't think how to say it *without* saying it.

'Ash, I want to leave,' she blurted out.

'What's that, Rennie?' Dear old Ash, she had really startled him. He appeared quite shaken.

'I want to leave, Ash. I've got to go,' she clarified, somewhat desperately.

'My dear, I don't understand. What are you saying?'

'I want to leave Barrindilloo, Ash. I want to go *now*. *Today*, if possible. Please can you arrange it, Ash? Please! *Please!*'

Rennie was gabbling. She must have sounded slightly hysterical, because Ash got up quickly and came around the desk to put a hand on her shoulder.

'Has something happened? You don't know what you're saying?'

'I do, I *do*. I want to *go*, that's all. I'm going anyway, aren't I, soon? Magda's happily settled, isn't she, so I was going to leave soon *anyway*, wasn't I?'

'Exactly, Rennie,' Ash agreed concisely, 'so what's the great hurry?'

'I want to go now, Ash, please.'

Ash pulled at his lower lip. 'You'll need to wait until Chad comes back, Rennie,' he pointed out reasonably. 'He's the boss, you know. He makes the decisions around here. We'll need to wait for him.'

'No! No, we needn't, Ash, truly. He won't mind, I know he won't. You could fly me out, couldn't you? The plane's there, all ready. I know you can fly a plane, because you told me so, remember? You used to fly one at the other Sandasen place – that other property – Koontilla, you said. You said you used to fly one there. *Please* take me out, Ash.' She was begging now, imploring. Even with her eyes, she was beseeching him to do it.

Ash shook his head slowly, shook it from side to side.

'I couldn't do that, even if I were to agree with you about it, which I don't. I haven't flown for years, and never a twin-engine like Chad's out there. It's a different technique entirely. I've never mastered asymmetrics, and if we happened to have an "engine out" we could be in real trouble. Chad wouldn't thank me for ditching his plane, or for breaking our necks, either! Anyway, I haven't a licence any more. Straight away I'd have the D.C.A. breathing down my neck if I took an aircraft up now.' Again he shook his head. 'It's best to wait till Chad gets back, Rennie. It'll only be a few more days, after all.'

Rennie's eyes were wide with quite desperate appeal.

'*Please*, Ash. I can't wait till then.'

'But why, my dear girl? What possible difference does a few days make?'

Ash was being soothing now. He was looking at her perplexedly.

'I want to go *before* Chad comes back,' she had to confess, in a tight little voice, and she was by now very, very pale.

'Why, though?'

How stubborn Ash could be when he wanted, how terribly persistent!

'Because I – don't want to see him again,' Rennie whispered – and then she sank down on the chair and covered her face with her hands.

For a time there was silence. Everything in the room was quite still.

'You're in love with him, aren't you?' Ash spoke so calmly that Rennie's head came up in surprise.

'H-how did you know?'

Ash patted her shoulder, gave her a kind, fatherly smile which was also vaguely apologetic.

'My dear, I've no wish to pry, but it was easy to guess. I realized it when you were dancing with him the other night. You aren't the first woman who's looked at Chad in that particular way. It was there, in your face.' A pause. 'I've been married myself, remember, Rennie. I've a daughter not much older than you. I didn't come down in the last shower, you know. A man gets to recognize the signs.'

'Oh, Ash!' In a way, it was an enormous relief, now that he knew. Now he would understand. Now he was bound to help her to get away, wasn't he?

'You will, won't you, now you know how I feel?' She had forced herself to confide in Ash a little more, in order to persuade him.

'I suppose I could drive you to Meridian in the Blitz,' he agreed reluctantly. 'Would that do?'

'Yes, that would help. I could make my way from there quite well,' she said eagerly.

'And what about afterwards, Rennie? What will you do then?' He fingered his chin unhappily. 'Will you contact your friend Stamford, or what? You don't know anyone down there, really, do you? You can't just go off into the blue.'

'Yes, I can. I'll be quite all right. I shan't see Keith again, not now, but I can take care of myself. I'm quite used to that. I suppose I shall g-go back to England.'

Away from this place, which she had come to love as she loved its master. She wouldn't be one of the ones who came back, one of the ones who 'crossed again'.

'Could we go today?' Rennie pressed him.

'Today! What about Magda?'

'I've been thinking about that, too. I think it's best if I say I'm going to the city for a few days. Chad can break it to her that I won't be back, once I'm gone a while. I mean, he was going to have to do that anyway, wasn't he, quite soon? It was going to crop up some time.'

'Yes, that's true.'

'I'll go and pack, Ash. It won't take me long.' There were tears in her eyes – tears of gratitude. Impulsively, she reached up and kissed him on the side of his kind, worried face. 'I'll never forget what you're doing for me, *ever*.'

'I'll go and check the Blitz and fill the jerry-cans.' He sighed, and followed Rennie out of the office with a marked lack of enthusiasm.

It did not take Rennie long to put her clothes into her case, but Ash seemed to take ages out at the garage. Or maybe he had gone to change his clothes. Murtie had told her that Meridian was the nearest town, but she had no idea how big it was, or if it was an important centre. It didn't really matter, anyhow, just so long as she *got* there.

She had to curb her impatience when Ash told her that

they would leave after lunch. Elspeth had half prepared it, and they had a long drive ahead of them, so it would be better if they had a meal first.

All through that meal he appeared preoccupied, so thoughtful that he made little attempt at conversation. A frown furrowed his brow as he ate in silence. Rennie felt guilt gnawing at her. Poor Ash, it was obviously on his conscience, what he was about to do. It was *worrying* him!

When they got up, he gave a wry smile. 'Well, Rennie, this is it. We'll need to hit the track, I reckon. We've just time for a farewell drink before we go.' He glanced at his watch. 'Where shall we have it, here or out on the veranda?'

'I don't think I want anything, thanks, Ash. We've just had lunch, haven't we?'

'Yes, I know, but we'll have one all the same. We'll be thirsty enough soon, and it's luck for the road, Rennie. It's the custom out here, you know, when friends depart. One likes to wish them well – wish them happiness – courage, too,' he added gently. 'I want one myself, so you mustn't be the one to break an old bush tradition. What'll it be? Whisky? Brandy?'

She wrinkled her nose. 'Not spirits, Ash.'

'A beer, then. I must say I could do with one! Two nice cold beers.'

He grinned with such enthusiasm that she really hadn't the heart to argue as he disappeared in the direction of the fridge, and presently came back to the veranda carrying a tray with a couple of tall, frothing glasses on it.

Ash passed her one, took the other, and set the tray on the floor beside his chair.

'I didn't fill your one quite so full,' he pointed out, as he raised his glass to her. 'Well, Rennie, this is one farewell drink that I wish wasn't necessary. I'm really sorry that you feel you have to leave in this way. Here's all the best, anyhow, my dear. We'll drink to future happiness, will we – and may all the present troubles soon be past! Bottoms up!'

He smiled encouragingly, dear kindly old Ash, and she

smiled bravely too, and kept pace with him as he downed his beer. It was pleasantly cold, and at the end of it there was still a tiny piece of ice left in the bottom of the glass, which she slipped into her mouth and allowed to dissolve.

'Ah-h!' he sighed appreciatively, leaned forward and put the empty glasses back on the tray. 'Now, you just sit there, Rennie, while I go and get the Blitz. I'll bring her round to the front when I'm ready. I'll give you a shout when it's time to say goodbye to Elspeth and Magda. O.K.?'

'Yes, all right, Ash.'

She relaxed against the canvas back of the deck-chair as he went off, and stared gloomily out through the gauze.

In front of her, beyond the veranda rail, were the sweeping lawns, the beds of canna and portulaca, the shrubberies, the tall ornamental trees that shaded the path. Barrindilloo. Home. Chard's home, not hers. Soon she would be leaving here. Any minute now. Leaving for good. For *ever*. Soon. Just as soon as Ash came back. What a long time he was taking at that Blitz! Not that she minded really. It was quite pleasant lying here in this deck-chair. They were surprisingly comfortable things, deck-chairs, if you got right down *into* them, like this. You could almost sleep like this.

Those cannas were sleeping, out there in the garden, and you'd have said even the trees were drowsing in the noonday sun. Their leaves were drooping in the heat, like the huge, floppy petals of the cannas. What exotic blooms those were, those cannas – and the colours – so *vivid* – they were blending now in an incredible way, before her eyes – the red and the orange and that darker red – all red – all dark – all black.

Rennie stirred. She might just as well snooze until Ash came back, and save her energy for that long journey ahead.

She had no idea what time it could possibly have been when she was roused by the sound of men's voices coming from the veranda outside her room. Funny thing, that –

she had thought that *she* was on the veranda outside her room, instead of here on her bed. Not that she minded, because when one felt as languorous as this, a bed was indubitably a very comfortable place to be.

'—going to have a clean-up. I've had the devil of a long ride in!'

'Never mind, you got here in time, although I must say I was beginning to wonder, when it got dark, if you *would* be in time—'

'In time for *what*?' That voice sounded deeply, crisply irritated. '*How* many did you say you gave her?'

'Only three, out of the number eight bottle.'

'Good God, you could knock a bullock-team out with that!'

'You gave her that much yourself, just the other day.' That voice was injured, no doubt about it. Rennie felt quite sorry for *that* voice! 'That's how I knew it'd be O.K.'

'The dose is two, you idiot. I only made it three because she was under stress. And with alcohol *too* – I mean, that in itself increases the effectiveness. It's a wonder you didn't think—'

'Well, I kept her here, didn't I, as you instructed? Keep her there till I come, you said. At all costs, you said. I don't care *how* you do it, you said. Keep her there, you said, even if you have to chain her to the veranda-post to do it!'

'Well?'

'Well, you can't tie a lovely girl like that up to a ver-anda-post. What would you have done yourself? You didn't seem too full of bright ideas when I called you up on the two-way. You only said what to *do*, you didn't say how to *do* it.'

'If I'd realized the possibilities in store, I'd have made a few suggestions, believe me!' Very grimly, that was said.

'Well, I don't reckon I did too badly. I can tell you one thing, for a while I was absolutely stumped, before this idea came to me. Anyway, playing Cupid's not my line.'

'O.K., we'll leave it.' A chair scraped. 'Pour me a whisky while I get a shower and shave, will, you, Cupid? And for Pete's sake keep those meddlesome fingers away from the medicine-chest while you're doing it!'

What a crazy, upside-down conversation! Rennie marvelled at the stupidity of it. Then, as two pairs of boots went away along the veranda and comfortable silence reigned once more, she went to sleep again.

When she woke, the first grey light showed her the outline of her window. Rennie got off the bed, surprised to find herself fully clothed, still dressed in the things she had changed into when she had got ready to go away to Meridian with Ash.

Something must have gone wrong somewhere, because she was still here, after all, and not in Meridian. Not even bumping over the plain towards it in the Blitzwaggon, but here, in her bedroom, at Barrindilloo. It was all very puzzling.

She groped for her sandals, slipped them on, automatically smoothed her rumpled head.

A sound on the veranda sent her to the window, peering out, and even as she turned, the light was flicked on, and Chad stood in the doorway.

Rennie simply put her hand to her throat and stared. Chad himself. She didn't even attempt to fathom how he had got here, or why – it was all a part of this crazy, mixed-up day. She just stood there, gazed dumbly at the tall, broad-shouldered figure in the narrow moleskins, clean white shirt, newly-polished boots, took in the weary lines that grooved his freshly-shaven cheeks, the watchfulness in his probing eyes, the cynical twist that pulled at his mouth. He looked pale, tired, a little grim.

'So, Renata. You thought you'd run out on me, did you?'

He took a step into the room as he drawled those words in a deceptively lazy way. She knew by now what that laziness could hide!

If he expected a reply, he didn't get one. Rennie couldn't speak. She found that she was trembling, ever so slightly.

She took her fingers away from her throat and clasped her hands tightly together in front of her. It was a gesture of appeal, of supplication, because she felt helpless to pretend any longer, and yet she knew she must. Oh, why couldn't he have let her go? Why couldn't she have got away?

'Why did you come back, Chad?' she heard herself ask finally, quietly, with a calm that surprised her.

'Why were you running away?' he countered smoothly, as he went on watching her in that curiously penetrating fashion. 'You don't intend to answer, I can see that.' His gaze sharpened. 'Or are you going to after all?'

He came over to where she stood, and now he was looking right down into her eyes. He still had that patient, controlled expression in his tanned face, as though he might be prepared to stand there for ever, waiting for her to reply. Rennie was aware of his nearness in a way that was torture. She could see the places where his hair was still dark-tipped with dampness after the shower, could catch the familiar aroma of his after-shave lotion; and that finely seamed scar that ran down the side of his stern face, on down his neck, to his collar, she could have reached out and touched it, he was so near; and that tiny muscle that flickered momentarily close to his jawline as it tightened just now, she could have smoothed away that tiny, almost imperceptible movement with one finger, without even moving from where she stood.

'I – no, I—'

She gave it up. What could she say that wouldn't be hopelessly revealing?

'What if I told you that the reason I came back just now was the very same reason as the one which made you try to run away?' he suggested carefully, and there were the beginnings of a smile in those green eyes as he said it. There was a message in them, those eyes, or at least, the *beginnings* of a message – the same message that had been there before – the one she couldn't seem to understand—

'I – I wouldn't believe you. It would be impossible!'

187

'On the contrary, nothing's impossible.'

'Please, Chad. I think this conversation is quite profitless.'

To her surprise, Chad agreed, somewhat grimly.

'Yes, I'm beginning to think that, too,' he said abruptly, and with one swift movement, he had taken her into his arms, imprisoned her there, and when she struggled, his hold merely tightened.

Rennie could only stay quite still, like a palpitating, frightened, captive bird. Chad's eyes were holding hers. They were mesmerizing her.

'Don't fight me, Rennie darling,' he was saying, and his voice was oddly husky, so that Rennie wondered if she could possibly have heard aright – 'Don't fight me any more, little sweetheart. I've had one hell of a trip in – I never thought I'd be in time.'

His lips were close to her ear, and she felt them brushing across her cheek. They were travelling, very slowly, very intentionally, towards her mouth.

'There are times,' Chad murmured thickly – and Rennie only just caught the words – 'when conversation can be *quite* profitless.'

And then he kissed her, very tenderly, very gently, after which he took her face between his hands, and looked right into her eyes.

'Well?' Chad was quizzical. 'Did you get the message *this* time?'

'Oh, Chad!' She melted into his arms again, ecstatic, only half believing even now. 'You called me Rennie – like my friends do,' she said, on a note of wonder.

'I called you "darling",' he corrected sternly, 'like mere friends don't – or shouldn't.'

'Rennie *and* darling. You – I – you've never called me that before!'

'Just once.' His mouth lifted lopsidedly, in that endearing way. 'But I couldn't expect you to remember the occasion, right in the middle of a water-course that had just come down a banker, when I was trying my best to keep my balance for both of us, and save us from a ducking.'

188

'But I did! I *do!*'

'You pushed me away.'

'*Him.* I pushed *him* away. I thought you were Keith.'

'You said his name, quite clearly.'

'*Did* I? I didn't know that.'

'That's why I went away straight after, once I'd made sure you'd be all right – to leave the field to that Stamford cove.' Chad grinned. 'It took more will-power than I ever thought I possessed, but you seemed to have made your preference unpalatably plain.'

'Oh, Chad!' She gazed at him helplessly, and her eyes were brimming with an emotion she could no longer hide – 'that's why *I* was going, too. Because of Leith.'

'Leith!' He was startled, it seemed, and not altogether pleased. 'What the blazes has she to do with it?'

'Well, I – I thought – I mean, I *knew* that there was this understanding between you.'

'What understanding?' He looked at her sharply, with an unwavering gaze, quite clearly puzzled. 'Rennie, what are you talking about? What was this understanding I'm supposed to have had? When, by word or deed, have I ever led you to believe that there was an understanding – an *insipid* word, that! Too insipid for *us!* – an understanding between myself and Leith? Have I ever said any such thing?'

'N-no, Chad.' He hadn't of course, had he, really? *He* hadn't.

'Has anyone ever said any such thing?' he insisted sternly.

'No, Chad, they haven't.' Rennie met his eyes as unwaveringly as he had met hers. There were times in a girl's life when she could afford to be generous, and Rennie knew that, for her, this was one of those times. She'd never tell, never. And some day she and Leith were going to be very good friends. Rennie was going to work hard at that friendship, because Leith was really a very nice person in many ways. She couldn't find it in her heart to blame her for what she had tried to do.

'Little goose!' He drew her to him and kissed her again,

and this time the tenderness got quite out of hand. It gave way eventually to a passion that left Rennie ecstatic and shaken – as shaken as Chad himself.

He put her from him, ran his fingers through his hair distractedly.

'Dear heaven, Rennie, what you've put me through! Understandings, she says! I've loved you, I've meant to have you, from the moment I set eyes on you, that night down there in the city. You tried to escape me then, and you had a go just now, too, and if it hadn't been for a bit of timely communication between old Ash there and me, I'd be having to chase all over the country, looking for you to bring you back! Well, I'm never going to let you go again, Rennie, do you hear? You're going to be my *wife*, and to hell with "understandings" and conventional delays while the lady makes up her mind! Darling, will you marry me?'

There she was, back in his arms, and Chad was waiting for her answer. He was looking tender and impatient and demanding, all at the same time.

'Whenever you say, Chad.' A dimple peeped furtively, as Rennie concealed a smile. This was probably the only time in his life that the boss of Barrindilloo station had ever deferred to anyone, and it was probably the only time in *her* life that he would defer to *her*! Rennie, curiously, didn't mind at all!

'Do you think Ash could give me away?' she asked meekly.

'I don't see why not. He'd better do something to make up for doping you in that atrociously ruthless fashion, hadn't he?'

'And Magda could be our flower-girl. She'd be sweet, wouldn't she, as a little flower-girl?'

'Mm.' Chad's eyes were on her face. It was doubtful if he was really listening.

'*Sweet*,' he repeated, in a tender, dreamy way.

'And could Murtie come, and all the rest? I really would like Murtie and Elspeth too.'

'Mm.'

'Chad, are you listening?'

'Yes, my darling little schemer, I'm listening, and the answer is yes. That wedding-day is going to be *your* day — *our* day — and you shall have it just whatever way you want it. And of course they'll all be there — Murtie, Harry, the lot. I couldn't get through a thing like a wedding without them, could I? It'll be worse than a bangtail muster! But after we're married, they can go off and paint the town. They can paint it red, or red, white and blue, for all I care — because I'll have other things on my mind, and so will Mrs. Sandasen.'

'Chad?'

'Yes, Rennie?'

'Chad, *I've* loved *you* for a very long time, too,' she confessed a little shyly, with her face pressed against his shirt. 'I've been thinking back, and I know now that that's what it all meant, all the time I was fighting against it. I've been so stupid, not knowing what it was.'

And Leith hadn't helped!

'And now? You're sure?'

'Quite sure.' She looked up at him, and Chad's eyes were crinkling in that greenly teasing way. His white teeth glinted in his teak-brown face as he smiled down tenderly, as if he had got *her* message too.

'Do you think we could have that wedding very soon?' asked Rennie, on a whisper.

And down at the creek, the kookaburras started chuckling, gleefully, jubilantly, triumphantly, telling the world that the spirit fires had been lit and that the sun would soon be up, and that it was time for all the other earth-dwellers to get up too. They were laughing-in the dawn of a brand-new day — a wonderful, new day that somehow belonged, almost exclusively, to Rennie and Chad.